Silver's Threads

Book 5

Other Titles by Penny Reilly

Silver's Threads Series

Book 1, Spinning Colours Darkly © 2012
Reprinted and revised 2013, 2014

Book 2, Grey Weavings © 2012
Reprinted and revised 2013, 2014

Book 3, Warp and Weft © 2012
Reprinted and revised 2013, 2014

Book 4, Silken Web © 2014
First Edition 2014, Reprint 2014

Forthcoming

Cloak of Magick Vol. 1,
Song to a Green Moon ©

Non-fiction

Little Magicks *…Nature Poetry* ©
Earth Rites *…the Way of All Magicks* ©

Silver's Threads

Book 5

Skeins of Tyme

Penny Reilly

ISBN 13: 978-0-9924759-5-6

Silver's Threads Book 5
Skeins of Tyme
© 2014 by Penny Reilly

Cover and interior design by Penny Reilly
Cover Art "Faerie Treasures" by Josephine Wall
Editor Christina Thorburn
Illustrations by Penny Reilly and jvoetsch@clipart.com

Penny Reilly
First Edition 2014

Printed in Australia

Dedication

I dedicate this book as officially taken from the
'to do pile' to the 'done pile',
...which is growing daily.

Special Acknowledgement

The beautiful cover art of this book, "Faerie Treasures" is by the extraordinarily gifted Josephine Wall. I am honoured to work with her creations …her art has constantly inspired me through the birth of five books; her paintings come to life for me as I write, whispering their Magickal stories; I only hope my words can do justice to her art.

Please visit Josephine Wall on her face book page

www.facebok.com/TheOfficialJosephineWall

…and her gallery www.josephinewall.co.uk

Acknowledgements

This has been an extraordinary two-plus something years of work throughout which the support from friends and my husband David has been wonderful. No books are born without the aid of family, friends, colleagues and ultimately, readers …on all counts you know who you are. I thank you all deeply for your support and faith in me to get the job done. To Tina my editor, Susan, Noelle, Kat, Tracy, Sonya, Rhys, Jo, Suzie and so many others, who read some of these pages as they grew and now as this series ends. Yet again, thanks go to my wonderful sisters and brothers at 'The Attic' for continued support, mutual brainstorming and a few giggles along the way; thank you Kim, Carole, Aynia, Stacey, Joanne, Nicky, Phoenix, Helen and Luke …good luck to you all in your own writing endeavours. Special thanks to the quiet, and not so quiet, followers of my facebook pages and my blog silversthreads.

Foreword by Penny Reilly

A book (or five) of this nature is a theme that grows, taking the writer to uncharted depths and into broad vistas. To write a fantasy that encompasses multi-layers of understanding and philosophy is no mean feat and at times an exhausting process. As the wheel turned for me, so too did the wheel turn within the web of the story; characters grew, changed, diminished, won and lost and at times, I was not sure where they led me.

Does Spirit have an agenda for a perceived 'higher' purpose or do they, as progressing souls on a journey of understanding, put their own ideas forward just as we do on our physical journey?

We forget that we are spirit as much as physical matter yet also 'eternal mind'. We have perhaps unknown agendas long determined to fulfil, not for our own personal gain as an individual 'person' but as an evolving entity searching for the truth of consciousness. Can we ever find it, does spirit self, soul self, the Littleshape ever truly 'know' the source of its existence or must it travel throughout the time space continuum in the search for its Trueshape? Its ultimate Soul self.

From a human perspective, we can only hope that it is an evolving experience for our species to find a rationale for being here. For otherwise we are indeed a lesser race; apart from the odd rogue or a bid for survival of the fittest in a dying breed, there is no other species that creates such mayhem in its own environment, particularly when we are completely reliant upon it.

Beyond the Gate Penny Reilly October 2014

...the story so far...

How much can one woman take? Samantha has crashed again and the group surrounding her struggle to remain strong in order to help whilst the search for Sybille continues. The outcome of the last rite leaves everything in uncertainty.

Three deaths have further added to the trauma of the times,: Annie Savage, Vanessa's mother; Nina and Magdalena. Yet joy mingles with tears as Alma and Maeve reunite as sister-friends and mother from another thread. Jamie and Maeve may yet rediscover their bond.

Callum, stronger than ever before, keeps his secret close to his chest but knows the time is approaching to reveal all ...he waits for Hercurin's signal and Vanessa keeps a secret she wishes she could shout from the rooftops.

Now Sam has vanished again, just as her shaper's bracelet is returned to her. What is this twisted thing called fate?

...the story continues...

Skeins of Tyme

Threads of Silver, silken fine,
Reweaves the web, all souls entwine;
A tapestry of life Divine
...upon the Skeins of Tyme

Silvern words, a promise spoken
What was lost is now re-woven,
In honouring life, the spell is broken
...to heal the Skeins of Tyme

She the weaver ...She the web
Fear's grip forever fled,
Unraveled now ...each soul
Each bright, untangled thread
...renews the Skeins of Tyme

Gold and silver intersperse,
The web of life and burst,
Like stars throughout the Universe,
Each delicate note ...a soul's rebirth
...upon the Skeins of Tyme

...Arianwen Isil'Lindir & Aithlin Farandir
...from the Skeins of Tyme

Prologue

The Wheel spins on …the moon, rises bright
…yet darkness prevails in the bounds of night
Sticky webs form and the innocent die
…leaving streaks of light across a blood red sky

Aerandir found himself back at the moment at Mabon, two years ago in human reckoning, when he'd first watched, sneering as the pseudo Wytches played their paltry, hierarchical games. He had observed from the edge of the forest on the Mount as Annie Savage stepped toward the balefire to catch, what at first appeared to be a falling spark, a firefly-like creature.

Since then, so much had changed; he had changed. It was the same moment but shifted, altered through his changed attitudes. He had waited for just such an opportunity many times in his mind as he raced to catch the falling creature. He forgot everything about not showing himself to the Onceborn, about not interfering at their human rites. There was nothing but the need to catch that falling spark of light. As he threw himself in front of Annie he faltered, unexpectedly seeing a face in the crowd that had not been there that Mabon night, Vanessa.

On the Lammas thread, Arianwen leapt toward Sam, seeing the fear in her friend's eyes. She heard in her head Sam's scream of, 'I can't do this Bethy. It has to end now, tonight,' and as Sam disappeared, she held out the bracelet that could help her friend make the natural shift, it was too late; Sam had no time to grab the proffered bangle. Arianwen was prevented from leaping after her as several pairs of strong hands held her back. Then Morgan shifted and flew, grabbing the bracelet in his taloned claws. 'I'll get her,' his words came to her on the wind. 'I'll bring her home,' then he too was gone, followed closely by Pwyll, Jamie and Tara.

Cal only had a moment to prevent Flora from blindly following. He heard Sam's scream and that of another; a piercing, terrified shriek as if from far away. The words **'Not again. Oh please, not again,'** echoed.

Helplessly, the rest of the group watched as their friends disappeared into the world between worlds.

Chapter 1
The Wheel Turns On

Lives within lives
…many twists and turns in time
…through the mists, lost in the rhyme.
Yet the way becomes clear
…when we follow what's most dear.
In our belly, in our heart
…not separate …nor yet apart

One week and another passed; the wheel turned. Life took on sameness except Sam, Morgan, Pwyll and Jamie were gone and not heard from since Lammas. All the talking, planning and performing of rituals seemed to be of no help whatsoever and those remaining were at a loss.

Max now spent most of his time with Lily at her shop, Greenman Ways, which was her home in Glastonbury. Robert was a great help, keeping them both focused and positive that things would unfold as they must and that worry was not going to help. Having him close all the time was a blessing for them and they encouraged everyone to meet there as often as possible. He was a steadying force in a world gone crazy.

Maeve took Alma back through the veil, hoping to find Jamie on the other thread but there was no sign of him and so they returned to Scathach's Hearth to resume a simpler, if somewhat harsher life.

They were inseparable, ever hoping Jamie would return but scared they might miss him if he returned to find them gone.

Maeve and Alma often travelled through Susan's portal painting at Greenman Ways to Springsmeet, bringing with them things Maeve had made for the shop, such as wands, Athame and some beautiful Celtic style jewellery. They never stayed long but one day, not long after Lammas, Bethan took Maeve aside.

'We need you here,' she said in her gently direct manner. We still have a business to run and with Sam...' she trailed of hesitantly, '... with Sam gone, we need an extra pair of hands. It's not fair that Vanessa should take it all on when she's still grieving the loss of her mother. Work may be a useful outlet but even so, she needs a little TLC right now. Jamie will know where to find you and Claire's going to look for Sam and the others in the Skeins. We need you here Maeve.'

Maeve felt Alma's hand grasp hers firmly. 'We can stay Lady Arianwen.' She said to Beth. 'I can help. I know how to polish the sparkly things in the cabinets, Rowan …erm Sam, showed me.'

Turning to Maeve, she said 'We can stay Mam, Da will find us here. We have to help and we still have something left to do. I don't know what, but I just know it.'

'Well,' said Maeve with a broad grin at her daughter,

'that's telling me then.' She hugged her little girl to her. Alma was the making of Maeve, Bethan thought. Her friend was more like the serious but fun loving girl she knew from years ago.

Alma laughed mischievously at them, her little face transformed with delight. 'I promise not to make the cauldron rumble but I can't promise the same of my friends,' she said with candid honesty.

'You can call me Beth here on this thread Alma. I know Arianwen is the greater part of me, but I'll still be Beth here, for now at least.' She fondly ruffled Alma's wild red curls, so like Maeve's, dreaming of the day she might have a little girl or boy of her own to love.

Alma, sensing Beth's thoughts through her uncanny knowing, hugged her fiercely and whispered a little song to her, *'When Beltane comes around and juicy fruits abound, He will come to you with white blossoms fair, to thread about your silver hair and to dance the circle round.'*

Beth laughed, '...and what would you know about such things little Alma?' who had the grace to blush.

'Oh, I peeked at Beltane,' she said blatantly, 'and I know what the goats and pigs used to get up to when spring arrived.'

Maeve, smothering a chuckle with her hand, didn't miss their interchange. 'All right then, I guess we stay on here, but I'll have to let The Cybil and Lady Scathach know,' said Maeve.

'I can do that Mam, I know the ways between.'

'Yes, and speaking of that Alma, we need you to show us the way to the cave where Rowan's bones are.'

'Okay,' Alma replied reluctantly. She didn't want to remember or go back to the places where she might run into M'lady, but she remained silent about that.

'There's no need for you to ever be afraid again, Alma.' Sensing her reticence, Bethan squatted down to be on eye level with the child. 'We'll never let her influence you again, we promise, don't we Maeve?'

'Absolutely, although I'd like to get my hands on her, personally,' Maeve said with a fierce scowl. 'There's a lot she has to answer for and I think it's only now we're beginning to understand just how much.' She stopped, seeing Alma shrink in fear. 'It's okay love,' she said to her daughter. 'Beth's right, she won't get anywhere near you again.'

Vanessa walked in at that moment looking drawn and tired. Flora was close behind her. After greetings and hugs were exchanged Alma excitedly announced they would be staying here more and that she would help in any way she could. The three women exchanged bemused glances at the enthusiasm and change in the little girl.

Vanessa smiled and handed her a sweet from the folds of her dress, much to Alma's delight, who glanced at her Mam to see if it was all right to eat it straight away.

Life, everyday life needed addressing: customers to serve; orders to fill, music to be played and sung (although without Morgan that was proving a little more difficult as it left only Beth and Vanessa in Unearthly Sounds.)

They separated for the day to go about their tasks. Vanessa went to reception with Alma tagging along behind where she could polish and dust the 'sparkly things' to her hearts content. Beth ascended to her studio to weave and Maeve withdrew to hers to draw up some designs she had in the back of her mind.

No one spoke of the next stage of the journey to find Sybille; they did not dare voice their fears that it might not be a possibility.

They were all to meet in Glastonbury at Robyn's farm. It was a good space for them to get together because of course, Robyn could not travel the Between, bound as he was to his land, just as Hercurin was to his. Robyn may have chosen to live a human life, sharing it with Sybille when he could but he was still what he was, a Greenlord and as such, could not travel far from the boundaries of his own being.

Chapter 2
Jamie's Journey

*Raven or owl ...fox or blue jay
...each is within ...find the key there today
When you remember ...when you awake
...who are you really ...what is your true shape?*

After Sam disappeared into the weave and knowing the winged shapers were better equipped to search for her than he, Jamie retraced his steps from the cottage, where Nina spent the remainder of her days, back to her father's house. Grief hung like a veil over the lovely, old building. It was as if the walled gardens were empty of life; not a leaf stirred on trees once alive with leaf-sprites.

Only the nature deva Nangini waited under the spreading nut trees near the house where Nina and Magdalena sat so often together in their last young years of life.

There was no sign of Eduard and the house appeared neglected and empty; he was no longer able to live in the place that had afforded him so much joy and eventually such pain. Nangini watched him, scrying where he travelled across the world in his search to find a semblance of peace.

Jamie changed to his fox form, crossing the courtyard in a few lithe bounds to scale the wall around the house, cat-like as a fox can be. Leaf litter had blown up against the doors and across the once clean-swept cobblestones and although it was spring here, the trees hadn't bothered to show their leaves or blossoms, perhaps in memory of the two young women who so loved their ancient boughs.

Changing again to his human form, Jamie quietly turned the doorknob and surprised to find it unlocked, paused when he heard movement inside. He entered quietly; not wishing to scare whoever was there, he closed the door gently behind him. He heard muttering as he approached the kitchen. Peering into the darkened room, he saw a woman sitting in a rocking chair before the old stove. She had the appearance of one who had once been large, but her flesh hung loose on her big-boned frame and grief hunched her shoulders. She mumbled to herself unintelligibly and buried her face in her apron, sobbing.

He was helpless to approach as he was a trespasser but his kind heart sent her waves of gentle energy and a brief gust of the woody fragrance Nina favoured toward the grieving woman. He heard Nina whisper, 'Nona, it's okay, shhh, I'm here, don't cry anymore,' and then he crept up stairs to Nina's chamber where he was not surprised to find that nothing appeared to have changed

Alma had told him where she had left the item he sought. It did not take him long to find it on Nina's dresser. Pocketing it quickly, he left as silently as he arrived. Nona appeared to be calmer and was feeding the fuel stove with kindling. Jamie breathed a sigh of relief that she was looking a little less distressed; he could still smell Nina's scent, but she was not visible, even to his keen sight and sharp senses.

Chapter 3

Untold Truths, Hidden Lies...

Lies become a web of fears
...that wraps a soul in a cloak of tears
Truth is the balm that soothes to heal
...but the power of lies has its own appeal

One by one Beth, Flo, Cal, Vanessa, Maeve and Alma made their way directly through the portal to Lily's and from there walked together to Robyn's through the late afternoon light, catching up with Susan and Alex on the way. Claire would make her own way through the aethers as she had left early to search for Tara, angry at her desertion of the group when they needed her most.

Jamie surprised them, turning up out of nowhere to grab Alma and dance a silly dance with her. He whispered to her under the cover of her giggles, 'I found it. It was just where you said it would be.' He patted his jacket pocket and Alma's grin deepened. Only Bethan, with her keen hearing, heard their exchange and wondered but Jamie would not reveal where he had been or what he had been doing.

Spring was showing her true colours; the hedgerows were blossoming and budding in green and white. Ostara approached and the roadsides were full of hyacinths, blue bells, wild daffodils and jonquils.

Bethan began to sing a song she had sung with Morgan and Unearthly Sounds and as she sang birds fell silent. '*The Seer's Isle, the isle of dreams hidden beyond the Mysts of Tyme, where beyond the lands of human schemes ...lies a land of great design*'.

'I remember this one,' said Vanessa as she joined in the second verse; it was the first time they had heard her sing since her mother's funeral. '*For deep within, the Magicks return, if you feel your heart race it's for this that it yearns. So wake up human child and before the year turns, feel the fire in your belly ...let it burn*'.

Shakily Flora and Maeve joined in, Alma too, surprising everyone with the sweetness of her voice. '*A coracle drifts across waters deep to the Seer's Isle the land within sleep. Where the Otter swims free; on the shore stands a Deer and the Raven flies beyond all mortal fear.*'

They continued walking and singing, laughing at Maeve's raw, husky sound. '*Avalon of the Heart in the swirling Myst the moist drops on your skin as soft as a kiss. Where the song of all Tyme is heard in the deep and the Mother calls to you in your sleep.*

Wake up human child come dance with the wind wake up and see where new life can begin. Feel the sun on your face and the breeze in your hair; wake up human child; let go all mortal care.'

'*For the world is renewing; if you wait it will cease. You will miss the Quickening of the Green Ways of peace. She has waited so long for you all to awake, so wake up human child for your own sweet sake.*' Jamie's deeper tones joined in on the final verse as he swung Alma up onto his shoulders, galloping like a wild pony, to her great delight.

On reaching the farm, Robyn greeted them warmly, ushering them inside. A spread of early berries, salads, cheeses and fresh baked bread awaited their arrival. Despite the air of seriousness each felt about the coming meet, Robyn provided a warm and welcoming space where for a little while they could speak of mundane matters. They settled to eat and share the news of the last few weeks with Robyn. Pwyll and Tara arrived together after Claire had found them combing the aethers for any traces of Samantha to no avail. It was as if something had swallowed her whole.

Pwyll looked exhausted, his gaze shifted to Tara in agitation as if he wanted to say something but was unable. Tara looked ruffled and unkempt in her human form, as if she had repeatedly run her hands through her tussled hair; it hung in greasy strands, unusual for the poised shaper they knew. Dark webbed lines appeared briefly on her pale skin. Alma withdrew from her rapidly; her sunny face fell into lines of fear. Teeth bared, her eyes widening, she met Tara's but Tara shook her head, preventing Alma asking the question, which she forcibly bit back.

Robyn approached Tara, looking searchingly but said nothing. Everyone knew something was terribly amiss but it was obvious that, once again, the humans would be the last to know.

Now that Morgan had gone after Sam, Lily and Max brought Honey to Glastonbury with them. She almost cringed as she walked up to Tara, sniffing her cautiously and whimpering. She then walked, stiff legged, back to curl her massive frame next to Max's chair although her amber eyes did not leave Tara. Honey lay shivering, even though Max scratched behind her ears and soothed her with gentle words.

'What's going on?' said Lily, moving to sooth Honey. 'What's frightening Honey, Tara? Where have you been? You look terrible. Have you seen Morgan?' Her words came out in a rush of indignation and pain.

Robyn pulled himself up to full height, appearing to tower over the diminutive Lily. 'Let it be Jaylily. There are things we may not speak of here, even if we wanted to.'

'But…' Robyn's raised hand silenced Lily before she could argue further. He beckoned Tara to come with him to his library. They left the room and no one moved for a moment, then they all began to speak at once.

Lily looked to Pwyll, 'Da, have you seen him?'

Pwyll shook his head sadly, clearly discomforted. 'No, I've been searching for your mother. She holds the key to so much.'

'What?' she screamed. 'You let my brother wander Goddess knows where while you're still searching for **her**!' She spat the word at him contemptuously. 'Have you still no care for him, for us? Has she ensnared you to such a degree nothing else matters to you?'

Pwyll made no reply but his silence gave them the truth of Lily's words.

Claire's face hardened, the realisation came fast. 'It's **her** isn't it Pwyll? After all these years, she still has you caught in her web.'

Claire's words resonated around the silent group.

'Did you say web?' Vanessa spoke up. 'Is this the same *web* that appeared on my mother's skin, the web of black we see through the forests and just now on Tara's face?'

Claire reached out to Vanessa, stroking her arm gently. 'Do you see what this *web* of lies is creating Pwyll? This isn't just your story to hide or tell; it affects every person in this room and particularly your children and Rowan.'

Pwyll remained silent, his eyes pleading with Claire not to speak but she turned to the room looking each of them in the face in turn. 'There is more going on here than I can possibly tell you alone. I need help with what I believe may be happening. I need to talk with 'The Cybil'. Maeve, can you take me to her, you and Alma?'

A small hand crept into Claire's, 'I will,' said Alma. 'Mam's needed here, but I will. Then I'll take you all to where Rowan's bones lie.'

Her little, freckled face was fierce with determination as she stood directly in front of Pwyll, who could not meet her eyes. 'You have to tell what you know, doesn't he Da?' turning to Jamie for support, who nodded his agreement. 'It's not fair that all these good people are left grieving their friends, **my friends** now, and family. Lily - her brother, Vanessa - her Mam, which hurts Flora to see her sister hurt'n,' her brogue returned as her voice shook and she held back the threatening tears. 'You hav'ta Pwyll, for Rowan and Morgan, Magdalena, Nina and her Da, Minhiriath, Aithlin, Aerandir and Arianwen,' she trailed off.

Beth knelt at Alma's feet. 'Mirdhaucha,' calling her by her Merrow name, 'what do the Elvenkin have to do with this, or with my mother?'

Alma gulped back her tears and fear. 'It's M'lady, Aelish, she's one of them …of you,' she corrected herself.

'Yes, we know but she's not really; she's Dark Fae.' Bethan struggled for understanding.

'Yes Lady but she wasn't always.' Alma collapsed in tears, throwing herself in Maeve's lap.

Beth's eyes took on a steely glint as she shaped, calling on all her latent power, she turned to Pwyll. Just at that moment Robyn returned to the room with Tara, who was looking restored to her usual bright self. Arianwen stood her ground defiantly as Robyn watched her. Silver horns slid from her forehead, her hair came alive with little Makers and elemental sprites. No one had ever seen her so strong and formidable.

'I am Arianwen Isil'Lindir and I will have the truth. Call my kin, Mirdhaucha and take me to The Cybil. No Robyn,' she turned to him, 'I will not let this farce continue. We all need answers and Sybille, Rowan and Morgan need to come home. For myself,' she hesitated, her gaze wandering to beyond the window as the glow of a fading sunset filled the room and she saw her kin gathering, 'I need the truth to my own mother's death, no murder; let's call it what it is.' With that she threw a cloak of Magick around her and vanished with Alma in tow. Her words echoed on the aethers as she called, 'Pwyll, since when do Elvenkin turn from light to dark and why and when did you become glamoured by such?' Pwyll did not reply.

'What did she say?' Susan said quietly. 'My friend Sarah was murdered?' Burying her face in Alex's shoulder, she stifled her sobs.

'Well?' said Lily but Pwyll, shaping to his Owl form, flew through the open window. No one made a move to stop him, but Flora saw the pain in her mother's eyes and the divided loyalties that had them all bound in the Skeins.

Vanessa stood quietly looking out into the darkening garden where a tall Fae with silver-streaked, jet hair stood waiting.

'Lle um cael i' onsint, Nessa. Amin cael sai a' onsint nan' amin le desiel a' vest amin lye il noste mori. Ta san kelvar il n'ataya lle.'

'You do have the answers in you Nessa,' he said in her mind. 'I have much to answer for but I am ready to admit that I did not know we are not born Dark and that it takes something terrible to alter us. I can't remember what it may have been but I'm willing to try that I may help, so that your mother didn't die in vain.'

Vanessa raised her hand in acknowledgment as he faded into the forest rim. Nina stirred for the first time since her sudden death, ready to help Vanessa find the truth of it all. Vanessa wore the key she had received as her Yule gift around her neck and wondered, not for the first time, what it unlocked. Perhaps Aerandir was right; perhaps it was for the little cottage where Nina had stayed. Vanessa also wondered what other secrets might be hidden there.

She asked Jamie if he would take her back there. He made no reply but merely handed her a small leather pouch; taking her arm he led her away from the chattering, fragmented group while she opened it. Inside was a small, burnished metal fox head pin. It seemed to move and sang a song of subtle power. There was pain and joy intermingled in its energy; it glowed briefly as she pinned it to her crop top beneath her shirt. It hummed gently, warming to her body warmth.

Nina stirred again, sighing; longing for the shape change to begin again. Vanessa's eyes widened as she understood the meaning of the gift. Nina sent her imagery of a journey, with Jamie in fox shape, through snow.

Vanessa's face lit up as she recognised the location of the cottage, but Jamie cut her off before she could speak of it.

He smiled, 'It was lost for a while. Alma took it back to Nina's father when I took her body home. I nicked it today from where Eduard put it, but he's gone travelling and I thought it needed to find its new owner. It's what Nina would have wanted; does want. I sense her in you Vanessa and yes, I'll take you there later after we finish here. It's not far at all,' he finished with a grin.

'Thanks Jamie, if I weren't scared of what Maeve would do I'd kiss you right now.'

'Well, a sisterly kiss is okay by anyone,' he said waggling his eyebrows at her as Maeve came over.

'Oh, beware this foxy-lad's charms Nessa. He's a dangerous sort for sure!' They hugged Vanessa between them, laughing.

Flora and Cal watched a little bemused at the change in energy, despite the bombshell Alma had dropped about the Fae not being born Dark. Everyone had assumed the Fae were two distinctly different races - Forest and Cave, but this assumption needed some revision in their minds. There was nothing more to do that night except dream of a final resolution to it all.

Vanessa sobered quickly. 'What about Alma, Maeve? Aren't you worried about her safety?'

'Of course I'm concerned Nessa, but if you knew what Alma's capable of! She's a match for anyone, although she freaked out about Aelish, she's very resilient.

She'd have to be after everything she's experienced, but let's face it, she's in good hands.'

'True but still, we can't afford any more of the team to go missing. It's hard enough keeping track of everything as it is. It seems the threads are entangling more than ever, rather than us finding ways to disentangle them.'

'I have a feeling we're about to make a break through,' said Cal coming in on the conversation. 'Something is changing and we're not letting even the cleverest or wisest get away with anything anymore. We're becoming strong enough to force the Fae and the Shaper's hands now. I'm over being 'just human' to them as if it was a lesser thing. I have ideas, but I'm not allowed to speak of them and it's really getting to me...' Cal trailed off as if he'd already said too much.

No one said anything, letting him recover for a moment. Flora took his hand in hers. 'Come on, let's go home, I'm too tired to think straight and so worried about Sybille and Sam it makes me feel sick.'

'Ah,' said Cal poker faced, 'that's pregnancy for you.' Flo laughed tiredly.

'Do you know I have trouble remembering all the babies I've helped deliver? What's happened to our lives the last two years? One day we may wake up and it will all have just been a bad dream.'

'Well, I for one don't mind really,' said Cal, 'because if this all hadn't happened I might not have found you.' There was a chorus of, 'Aawww,' at Cal's words.

Chapter 4
Resolutions, Memories and Dreams...

Where do you go in your dreams?
Are you sure you're awake?
Do you follow your heart
...or react for reacting sake...
Where are you when you are dreaming?
Is it a peaceful place?
Do you travel to the lands of beauty
...to a sacred greening space?
How do you feel in the morning?
Are you fully here
...or are you really still dreaming
... 'til small whispers of truth appear

After returning home through the portal the group scattered. Lily and Max offered a everyone a hot drink before they left but they were all too exhausted, just needing space to think and hopefully find solutions in sleep.

Cal, Claire and Flora brought Susan and Alex back through the veil, who left straight away for Springsmeet. Jamie brought Maeve and Vanessa. They arrived at Covenstead edgy and confused with all the happenings of the evening.

Before going up to bed, Flora questioned her mother. What was happening? Who was Pwyll's wife? What was meant by the Dark Fae not being born Dark?

'It's a long story Flo but it's time everyone knew the history of the shapers and their battle with the Dark Fae, Aelish in particular, but it's a long story and I'd rather get into it when everyone's around. It's really not something that can be told in a few sentences.'

'You're sounding like Tara now,' Flora grinned.

'Well, we're all shapers Flo, you included!'

'Okay mum, let's leave it for tonight.'

Claire kissed Flora on the cheek and calling out goodnight to Vanessa and Cal, went to her old dairy conversion on the hill near the Grove.

The Grove was alive with activity. Mabon was a couple of weeks away and Claire paused to think about Annie and the Mabon Rite on the Mount that had gone so tragically wrong for her. She heard the low hoot of an owl and hoped it might be Pwyll, but it was a barn owl out on its nightly hunt. No matter her anger at Pwyll's behaviour she still longed to spend time with him, to catch up on all the years. His story was a tragic one, not all of his own making.

Moths flew in the solar lamps set around her home and the owl was an opportunist. She thought briefly she might shape and hunt with the little-kin but no, she was just too tired and so headed for a hot bath and bed.

Claire dreamed of a huge owl that flew in through the window. She smelt his musky feathers and in her owl form, she fluffed and preened her own as he nodded and bowed in the mating dance. She awoke, tears on her cheeks and one long flight feather, lay on her pillow.

Since Morgan had gone after Sam and now Beth with Alma, Jamie and Maeve went to Wells to Beth's little cottage. Springsmeet or Covenstead were both options, Maeve having her space above Earthly Rites, but somehow the thought of the tranquillity of the forests at Wells called to them and they knew Beth would not mind them using the space Max had renovated in the old stables.

Their relationship, old in terms of other threads, was very new on this one. There was much to discover about each other and Maeve, still quite innocent in her sexuality, was finally ready to experience what it meant to love. She remembered clearly the Beltane Eve on another thread when they had danced the maypole round, finding their way to a quiet thicket to begin their life together and the eventual birth of Alma, conceived on that night.

She had told Jamie and he found it incredible that a woman as lovely as Maeve could still be untouched, but she explained her past and the men who had passed through her mother's life. Now Maeve was finally ready and on this golden, autumn night it was time for them.

Bodies joined, moving in the ancient dance, they melded heart and mind. There were moments Maeve was unsure whether Jamie was in fox or man form, the hair on his chest felt at times like the pelt of a fox.

That night Maeve dreamed she was back at the Beltane bonfire and felt the seed of their child take root to grow in her belly. She relived the birth, the loss and the eventual death to this world of the little girl they named Alma, whose joy and pain took her searching deep into the heart of underground caves filled with crystals and bones.

At Covenstead Vanessa made her way slowly upstairs, reluctant to be alone although she knew Cal and Flo were close in their own bedroom. She could hear their murmured tones as they readied for bed, Cal's deep chuckle and Flora's sighs of pleasure.

She stuffed a pillow over her ears, not wanting to hear them, as a strange and unknown longing rose in her. Music came from the forest, haunting and gentle. Aithlin she thought but then no, this was a different sound; it held a deeper throbbing rhythm that matched the longing she felt. Vanessa remembered getting out of bed and opening the window to listen to the strains of music, then she woke in the morning with a song on her lips that she knew would be something to work on with Morgan. As she climbed out of bed, drawing back the curtains to a frosty autumn morning, she crooned the words quietly…

'I'm not all I seem, let me into your dream …I'll show you the ways Between time but to follow me there; first come to my lair …and trust me to answer a rhyme. Ask me all you

will, I have consummate skill ...to travel all threads of Her song. Remember in truth, it is all by your will ...you learn which tone's right, which sings wrong. As the way becomes thin ...come follow your kin ...as they tread the roadways Between, for you're not all you seem and if you enter my dream ...I'll teach you to shapechange your skin.'

In her dreams she'd been running, a small fox in the snow. She shifted form on reaching a little house in a clearing where the music sang strongly in her blood. A tall Fae waited in the snow-covered forest on a hill near Glastonbury.

Chapter 5
Pwyll and Claire ...early days

Lives within lives ...many doorways of the soul
Even those in disguise lead you home, make you whole
We are not always kind, when we're troubled of mind
...but in truth it's a game, we're all one, all the same

Pwyll couldn't remember a day when he hadn't longed to touch her. Despite a friendship that he may damage by that need, he loved Claire Jenkins. She was married and although he sensed not entirely happy was at least content, particularly now that she was pregnant with her first child.

Harry, Claire's husband, was a strange and somewhat cold man. He appeared to be devoted to Claire on the 'public face' level, proud of her beauty, her skill in the complex work she did and yet Pwyll knew he was a cold and controlling man, which thankfully Claire was able to temper with humour and her ability to be a free spirit. Recently however, Pwyll had seen stress lines form on Claire's smooth skin; her due date was near and now that she could no longer work at the digs she loved, those lines were become deeply etched; shadows underscored her beautiful amber eyes.

Apparently, Harry had not wanted children. What he did want was a wife who would be at home every day;

there to serve dinners for groups of select people who would help establish his name in the world of surgeons. There was no doubt he was a brilliant man, but Pwyll had known him when he was an advocate for melding western medicine with herbal lore and homeopathy, chiropractic care, massage and meditation. He couldn't pinpoint exactly when it had changed, unless it had only been an act in the first place. As to knowing what manner of being Claire truly was, well at first Harry had seemed to be open to her declaration that she was a Shaper; a creature so ancient in origin it defied description. When given the opportunity to see her shift and to see Pwyll able to travel with her the rot set in. He pretended open-mindedness, but this too was a guise to hold onto Claire and to change her, but she was strong.

Now, with Claire's pregnancy blooming, Harry was leaving her alone more and more, just when she needed nurturing as a mother to be; reassurance that all was going to be okay with their marriage. Pwyll was not so sure of the latter and secretly lived in hope he would be more than just a friend to Claire, one day.

Susan Fenner was her closest friend, other than Sybille Maddison who was a little older than they were. Susan and Claire had gone to school together, growing up in the same leafy Melbourne suburb and then on to Uni, Claire to study Archaeology and eventually Anthropology and Susan art history and fine arts. They had been inseparable in those growing years and finally shared their rather 'different' origins to most, which is why Susan was astonished when Claire had met and married the rather charming and brilliant but coldly calculating, Harry Jenkins.

Now Susan sat with Pwyll and Claire as Claire began to show the first signs of labour; her baby was on the way.

They hustled Pwyll from the room at the birthing clinic. Claire asked him to keep trying to call Harry as the hospital had been unable to reach him and his child was not waiting for him to make an appearance.

Long before Harry arrived, Claire gave birth to a daughter she named Flora, after the Goddess of growing things. Tara appeared in a flurry of feathers and lacy black flounces to see the new addition to the Shaper-kin. Sybille drove from Covenstead as soon as the phone tree kicked in and Alex, Susan's husband, paced the floor outside the birthing room.

As a father of two, the elder his biological son Max and the younger their adopted little girl Bethan, he had sympathy for Claire's situation. He and Susan were closer than ever after the tragic circumstances that had brought their little girl to them. Harry was not a man Alex trusted.

As Claire gave birth the friends arrived. Claire, recovering quickly, held her daughter in her arms as they gathered. She asked Pwyll with sad eyes where Harry was; he shrugged and shook his head.

No one had reached Annie Savage, who put in an appearance shortly after Harry finally arrived and the others had gone home.

While his wife was in labour Harry was not in surgery where everyone thought he would be but rather in the bed of Claire's *friend*, Annie Savage. Cloaked in the devious Magicks of Aelish Farandirim, of which neither were aware, he found her irresistible and their affair had been going on since first Claire became pregnant.

There was no way Aelish would let Harry be with Claire to witness the birth of his first child. Annie, unaware of anything amiss, was vane enough to believe he wanted to be with her rather than his pregnant wife.
Already, the Skeins of Tyme had become, entangled to the point where the difference between truth and fantasy was unrecognisable. Would Annie have acted differently had she known?

Chapter 6
Annie and Harry

Caught in a web of entangled skeins
…unaware of the hand that held the reigns
Ego bound, the light grows dim
…for the one who betrayed her friends and kin

As a young woman, Annie Savage was vain but she was a very attractive person. Men flocked to her but women, although they loved her friendship and somewhat abrasive humour, never completely trusted her alone with their partners.

Susan, Claire and Annie were a close trio; the two childhood friends met Annie at Uni and fascinated by her relaxed and confident manner, or so they thought, made her their icon for stylishness. Her sultry Italian looks and style drew men like a magnet.

After their Uni days were over Susan became an acclaimed talent in the field of art and Claire in her chosen field but Annie had still not settled for any career that meant she would use her considerable skills in clothing design. Surprising them when she focused on accounting and business management; on completion she began working for Sybille, just seven years her senior. It meant she would move to Springsmeet where Sybille had set up her dream business in the then 'New Age' market. Sybille, being Sybille, knew there was nothing new under the sun, merely recycled ideas that suited the coming generation more than séances and backroom mediums.

Annie settled quickly, finding a cottage in walking distance to Sybille's thriving business where she found her niche and began studying the Old Ways, all-unaware under the influence of a spiteful spirit. She was delighted when, every year or so, Sybille began making trips on sabbaticals and writing retreats as her volumes became *the books* to read on new theories in meditation, the inner search for self and eventually on the practices of the Old Ways.

Annie would daydream that the business was hers and didn't correct customers when they assumed it was true. She went from strength to strength for several years, making herself indispensable in the day-to-day aspects of running a real business.

When Sybille returned home from one of her trips away, this time it had been to Glastonbury to give a talk on her latest book, she found Annie somewhat distressed but no matter how much she coaxed her to share what was wrong she met with resistance.

With something like fear in her eyes Annie said snappishly, 'I'm just tired is all; I need a holiday.'

'Why didn't you say, Annie?' Sybille said kindly. 'Take whatever time you need.'

'Well, I need a while. I have to go to Italy. My mother is unwell but she won't travel back. She never returned after visiting my Grandmother and after Gran passed she stayed on. Now she's sick, I don't know if she'll ever come home and there's no one else who has the time to look after her needs fulltime. I'll have to give you notice Sybille; I'm sorry to leave like this, but I don't know when I'll be back either.'

Sybille knew there was something else Annie was not saying but let it go at that. She had her suspicions that there was more to it than an ailing mother but couldn't quite put her finger on it. 'I'll manage Annie,' she said. 'Rose is back from the UK so perhaps she'd like to step in while you're gone. You know you'll have a job of some sort waiting for you, don't you?'

'Thanks Sybille,' was all she said before busying herself with the rosters for the team of readers for the coming months. 'The more I get done for at least a couple of months the easier it will be for whoever takes over from me.'

Rose Dane took over in Annie's absence, which turned out to be over ten months, and in the interim much changed. Annie never spoke of her time with her mother, who had given her enough money to pay off her little house in Springsmeet, except that she would be commuting while she was staying at her mother's house in Melbourne until it was decided what her mother wanted to do with it.

Never at any time did Annie mention that she'd been pregnant with Harry's child. Although she had been to Italy, she returned for the birth so that her daughter would be an Australian citizen. None of her friends, especially Claire, knew of her pregnancy or betrayal; not even Harry.

Under the cover of looking after her mother's affairs, she raised her little girl as best she could in secret while working part time for Sybille. She knew visits from Springsmeet would be seldom and made elaborate excuses of unavailability when anyone mentioned a drive to Melbourne. She felt relatively sure even Sybille's sharp intuition suspected nothing.

When Vanessa was school age, she spent most of her life at boarding schools while Annie returned to live in Springsmeet, taking back her full time job with Sybille as Rose moved back to the UK to help her daughter, pregnant with her first child.

Everything appeared to be falling into place and Harry returned to visit Annie regularly when she returned to Springsmeet. She refused to see him in Melbourne, with the excuse that she was scared someone would catch them. Although a large city, there was always the chance of bumping in to people who knew both Harry and Claire, but he was more nervous of someone seeing them together in Springsmeet and so their affair drifted.

As years passed the daughters of Claire and Susan played, went to school and continued the cycle of growing up, leaving home and finding their way until their own journeys with Sybille began.

Sybille had become an Aunt not long after Flora was born and was surprised her sister was happy for Samantha to visit and even stay for school holidays as the little girl grew. She wondered if Sam's parents knew the truth of her ancestry, but this eventually became evident as they started taking Sam to a hypnotherapist about what they called her 'strange little ways.'

Chapter 7
Pwyll and Aelish

When Pwyll thought back over the years he had trouble remembering how or even when he had met Aelish. He remembered a forest glade, sitting in his human form beneath a tree and thinking about Claire, whose motherhood role meant he now saw less of her.

Flora was six. How time had flown but, due to his dislike of Harry, Pwyll had only seen Flora on occasions such as birthdays and Sabbats. He was careful not to show himself as a shaper, although the smart little girl would often look at him strangely as if seeing more than she should.

Now, sitting beneath those same trees, he felt disempowered, lesser, as he considered the damage his wife had wrought. He considered how his children had suffered through her blatant neglect and he, unaware, had been equally guilty as he spent his time searching for a woman without whom he believed he could not exist.

How rude the awakening had been when the glamour had lifted and he saw her for what she truly was, a

Dark Fae, hell bent on killing or maiming any shaper who crossed her path.

He'd been so enamoured, so under her spell that he had put his children at risk from their own mother. It was, in fact, a blessing she had left them and he would soon tell them so, but now it was important he find her and have her brought to justice by the Elders of the Fae so that they might bring Sybille and Sam home.

Time seem to warp as he followed the twisted pathway of his thoughts back to the moment when he first set eyes on Aelish Farandirim. She had been standing in a sunlight filtered forest glade but she seemed untouched by the light; a dark nimbus hung around her like a cloak of mist and a glow about her gave her an unearthly beauty. Slender, dark haired and milky skinned - she reminded him of Annie Savage somewhat, although Annie's colouring was warmer toned.

She watched a deer that wandered in the dappled light, bow drawn back as she focused unerringly on her target. He warned the deer by intentionally snapping a twig on the ground. 'Since when do the Fae eat meat,' he said to the Fae.

She turned and all semblance of beauty fled as she snarled, aiming her arrow at him instead. He didn't flinch though, merely walked towards her, as a rabbit, caught in headlights would. He met her dark amethyst eyes and was lost as her glamour reassembled itself to the first impression he'd had of pale beauty. She smiled and he could no longer remember the deer or his question to her as she dropped her bow, walking toward him with sultry grace, to take his hands in hers.

Later he had woken to feel a wet tongue on his face as the same deer returned to the glade, rousing him from a dark, enchanted sleep.

He woke, knowing his wife Aelish would be waiting for him at home and that they had two children, Morgan sixteen and Lily just eleven years. Memory rushed back into him of the years since their births, forever searching for Aelish when she would disappear again, right up until she gave birth to each of their children. She had remained, tending them perfunctorily but without warmth or tenderness, only to vanish again for days on end leaving him to feed and bathe them until Morgan was nearly seventeen and Lily twelve.

Then Pwyll's need to find Aelish, at first an ache of longing, became raw anger and he left his children alone, handing the burden of raising Lily to a boy barely a man. No wonder they had been so bitter on his return but at least perhaps there would be some understanding now they had witnessed the power of Aelish's glamour after Annie's death. He could only hope and long for forgiveness; he a Shaper, a Firstborn, duped by a Dark Fae.

Shaking himself from his reverie, Pwyll shifted to his Owl form effortlessly; light gleamed from his bangle of power as he flew above the canopy of trees following the sticky shifting threads of the weave.

Chapter 8
Autumn Light

All that you say is heard by the birds
...have a care believe me they hear your words.
All of your thoughts and all of your dreams
...for birds are not all that they seem.
They're the Lady's little Magicks, the Fae in disguise
...look closely ...you'll notice
...it's hidden, deep in their eyes

Flora stood at the kitchen window, her hands still, the dish she held forgotten. She watched the passing nature sprites gathering in agitation. They searched continuously for Sam and would not listen when told no one knew where she had gone.

Careful not to startle her, Cal took the fragile glass dish from Flora's hands. She blinked as if coming back from a long way away. Feathers rustled somewhere in the room and he caught a fleeting glimpse of several small birds, their attention riveted on Flora.

'Flo,' he said gently with a wry smile, 'you have company.'

Turning to where he indicated, she saw a line of wrens, robins, finches and other small birds assembled along the backs of kitchen chairs and on any available surface that afforded a perch.

'Ah,' she said, smiling at him. 'They're everywhere. I try to get them to speak with the leaf sprites, but there seems to be a communication barrier. Perhaps only shifters speak 'wrenese.'" She giggled again, but Cal could hear a trace of hysteria in her voice. Flo, his lovely girl, was struggling constantly with the loss of her friends. She and Sam had become so close and it was only due to Sybille she was where she was today. Cal knew she would trade it all to have them both safely home.

Cal exchanged looks with Claire as she walked into the kitchen, shaking his head a little, his pain clear to her. She always thanked the Lady that Cal was in her daughter's life. If nothing else, this was a joy to watch unfold and now Flo was pregnant, blossoming despite her pain.

After the Lammas Rite she'd remained steady until the realisation hit that Sam was gone. No trace remained and even Claire had been at a loss to console her.

'But Mum,' Flora had cried, 'is everything we're trying to do to no purpose? Two years, **two years**,' she repeated, her voice rising, 'and nothing has given us even a glimpse that we might bring Sybille home.' They held her, while she cried.

Pulling herself together, she looked at both of them as if reading their thoughts. 'I know! This isn't good for the baby.' Cal and Claire didn't argue with her.

Now she stood, hands clasped over her already mounded belly, looking at the birds quizzically. 'How did you all get in here,' she asked the closest one perched on the kitchen table. 'If you're not shifters then where did you come from?'

Immediately, at apparently the right question, the bird shifted, becoming a small female Fae; not one Flora had ever seen before.

'*Amin hiraeth lye na a quel nauva. Amin nae lei nauva saian sinome. Uuner uma n'ala. Sybille ilyanemie quenne yassen lye, on aie vasa. Re chebin vama tuulo 'Tel Shee'*, it said. Flora could hear the translation in her head from her familiar spirit Bridd.

'We are sorry, we should not just barge in, but you see, we have always been here, it is just that no one has actually been able to see us before now. Sybille always chatted to us; fed us scraps and crumbs from her table and kept us safe from 'The Cat.'

Flora, knowing they meant Morgana rather than Teddy, smiled but made no reply, waiting for the Fae to finish.

'We are here to help but being the smallest of the familiar spirits we often get forgotten. We are, however, able to shift between the realms rapidly and silently. We are the messengers for humankin if they care to listen. Now Bridd,' she called Flora by her Shaper name, 'we can show you the ways through the veil to where we believe Rowan may be.'

'Really?' Flora said, excitement rising, 'When? How? What do we need to do?' her words tumbled out rapidly as she considered the possibility. 'If that's so, can you also help us find Sybille?'

'This is another matter, but we are eager to help. After all, she is our friend but this is a strange thing between Fae and humankin, whom we don't always trust.'

'What can we do to help?' Claire asked as the small Fae came closer, gazing at her with intensity. Claire didn't flinch, nor did Cal as their scrutiny shifted in turn to him.

'You know where Sybille is,' they said to Cal, who blushed when he saw the shocked expressions on Claire and Flora's faces.

'I may,' he said quietly, 'but I'm under oath not to repeat what I know or who told me.'

Claire and Flora looked at him reproachfully and he wanted to tell them but his tongue cleft to the roof of his mouth when he tried.

'Ah,' said Claire. 'Now I know exactly what Beth meant when she said she wanted to say things, share what she knows but is unable to form the words.'

Cal let out a sigh of relief. 'Yes,' was all he said as he felt Flora's arms wrap around him.

'Gather with us as the season changes again, Bridd and we will do all we can to help in the final Rite to find Rowan and when we find her you will find Sybille.' With a rustle of feathers and a sweet chiming call they vanished.

Flora, Claire and Cal felt a surge of hope. Finally, perhaps things were shifting in their favour. Mabon - autumn equinox was on the way, Ostara - spring equinox in the UK. More than two years had passed since Sybille vanished and they realised Sam had disappeared at exactly

the moment Sybille had, Lammas night. They had no
idea what the Lady asked of them as the Wheel turned
again or how they would make sense of the tangled
threads.

Chapter 9
Beth

We walk the Wildlands of the Between
...we search each being for a heart that's seen
...to care about life and a love of the Green
...only then do we share our knowledge; unseen

Beth sat in filtered moonlight, her Uilleann pipes silent across her lap. Winds blew gently through the open doorway and despite the cold it no longer affected her as it once would have.

Since 'becoming', she couldn't remember when she last felt the cold or heat, in all its Australian intensity. It would be so easy, she thought, to step from her Littleshape into her Trueshape and remain merged with all she was across the threads of lifetimes. There were answers she needed to find – Sam and Morgan; Sybille, where were they now? Often she felt she knew others knew but, as she had established before, until the words were ready to form and the moment true, such words would not come.

Her journey with Alma seemed like a dream and no one actually understood the concept, even after everything experienced, of a Tyme before time when the Firstborn walked the earth. She knew they did in theory but still she didn't know how to explain the concepts of everything being now.

As a Firstborn of the Fox Goddess Jamie knew and Nessa had a good understanding through her aspects and ancestry. Claire and Flora also, although Flo struggled at times with her own ancestry, which was probably a product of pregnancy hormones clouding the issue. It would appear her friends were becoming exhausted and in part almost ready to give up; give in. She feared they would fall asleep, like the Onceborn, return to innocent ennui, which would mean Aelish had won. She refused to let that happen and was greatly appreciative of Maeve, whose growth was exceeding her own expectations.

Sighing ruefully, Beth put her pipes aside. It was useless to attempt any new pieces, although she could see the notes; coloured pathways, they became tainted by black, sticky coils that changed their brightness to cacophonic chords of twisted, blighted darkness.

She wished, Morgan and Pwyll were there, Tara even; to help her find the notes to heal what needed healing. The song of life was dying; sadly, most Onceborn would continue on their way without noticing the changing seasons or the natural rhythm, which gives all things birth and life. After all, they had created a plastic coated existence, which took eons to break down in nature, even with Her tenacity. Was nature finally beaten she wondered? Fear hitched her breath, a strange twisted thing, glimpsed in peripheral vision.

Stirring, stretching she looked out at the beautiful natural forests of the Victorian highlands; Manna Ash,

Acacias, Eucalypts and Sheoak interspersed with latter day exotics, all living cheek by jowl without complaint. Native birds didn't worry if the hollow trees they found to live in were of European heritage; food was food to them, after all. Nature was an opportunist; if something healthy took hold and spread, it was simply nature's way. Only humans, having planted non-indigenous species in the first place, complained.

She breathed quietly; small creatures crept silently out of the forest, hares and rabbits along with echidna, tiny potoroos and marsupial mice. A hush fell as the forest and all its creatures held their breath …He was coming. Standing rapidly, she moved through the open doors to wait. One moment there was only the hushed forest; then there He was, taking shape from light and shadow; redolent of earth spice, breath from the breeze; fire from the last filtered rays of sunshine …Hercurin; his song rang bright through the evening…

'Fire burns in the core of me, running through the earth, through every tree.

Air breathes through me and all sentient ones, vibrating the fires; drumming the heartbeat drum.

Water moves me, deep and slow; languorous thoughts ebb and flow, from roiling wave to still deep calm, water soothes; a fragrant balm.

Earth holds me tight in her embrace. All things move across her face.

Beth transformed in an instant; horns reaching from a moon-white brow; tendrils of hair - twisting silver skeins, writhed, alive with shining creatures as they braided, tending the shining strands. A breeze lifted her soft-layered clothing of autumn colours, making the beautiful, woven textures into a swirling kaleidoscope of leaves and webbing.

She stepped toward the Forest Lord, their hands entwining; no need for words as brow to brow they communicated their song-thoughts in notes that had the Onceborn stirring in their beds, reaching, questing with dreaming minds for the source of such harmony ... unwritten notes of bliss escaping.

Hercurin showed Arianwen the next stage of the journey she, in her Bethan aspect, must take with her friends.

'Samhain,' he whispered. 'It must all be done by Samhain eve,' before embracing her in his warm musk scent to carry her to their forest bower.

Chapter 10

Eduard's Story

A man whose life was a lonely place
…until the moment he saw her face
…but then lost he became, alone and adrift
…the Lady is gone but she left a bright gift

 When Eduard first held his newborn daughter he marvelled at the fact she was so small, barely filling his hands. There again, her mother was a tiny thing and La Stregga had been concerned that the baby would be too big to bear naturally. Somehow the balance held and Nina Giraldi was born tiny but perfect, her features replicating those of her mother.

He tried to remember the events of the previous years before Aelish had somehow arrived in a flurry of busy hands and eager mouth, declaring she was a wealthy young woman of a titled house. He often wondered what the name of her father had been.

She had an air of innocence combined with a knowing way about her. He was indeed shocked to realise that she was no innocent on her wedding night and was, for the times, out rightly wanton.

Previously Eduard was a man of little passion, his interests being for the new science of alchemy and for the Old Ways of La Stregga. Aelish had certainly helped him to find his way around sexual passion and at times he shocked himself when he answered her every need with another of his own, unsought or even barely imagined before.

Everything changed after Nina was born. Aelish would disappear more often to who knew where. Eduard hired a Nona to help him raise his little girl. Nona doted on his child and although she was stern and taught her discernment in right from wrong, she was an active guiding force for a little girl who increasingly missed her mother but in turn was fast forgetting her face. She often asked Nona her mother's name, where she was and when she would be back.

A puzzled frown creased her little brow as she fought to remember but soon all thoughts of her mother faded as she grew to adolescence. On the day of her first blood, Nina became so ill and frail that Eduard sent for the Dottore to tend her. She had lost so much blood that it made no sense to Eduard they would consider bleeding her with leeches and so he called on his old friend La Stregga. She gave Nina an herbal tincture to help recovery from the blood loss and resulting anaemia. Slowly Nina returned to reasonable health, although each month the pain of her bleed would make her take to bed for a few days.

Even Eduard knew this was not normal for a young girl's monthly courses but he remembered the amount of pain her mother had experienced before and after Nina's birth. She had banned Eduard from her bed and all pretence of intimacy vanished, as did she eventually.

He educated Nina as she grew, for although her health was delicate she had a bright and eager mind. La Stregga would visit often, teaching them both the way of the Crooked Path and of the signs and answers nature would show them if they had the eyes to see. Astrology, alchemy, plant, bird and animal familiar spirits; nothing was left out as Nina studied and her father everything imaginable but still she battled recurring ill health.

Eduard sought help from La Stregga. He had long since made a chart of Nina's astrology and was horrified to see that his daughter's life was not to be of long duration. He was a man with a brilliant mind but he was open to anything that would keep his daughter alive and happy. If it meant selling his soul he would do so willingly.

Slowly but surely, as the glamour of Aelish faded, Eduard realised what manner of creature he'd taken as his wife, having refused to listen to La Stregga's and even occasionally, Nona's doubts. Now there was no room for doubt as he watched his little girl grow and eventually fall so ill she fell into a coma-like state.

Aelish returned once, only briefly. He remembered seeing her face on the edge of the circle La Stregga had cast when they had petitioned the Gods for Nina's life. He felt her hostility and knew his love for his daughter had been the undoing of his marriage. Aelish was not one to share anything or anyone she'd claimed as hers.

Despite their efforts, Nina improved but then succumbed to the sleep that should have meant her death approached. Night after night Eduard would hold vigil at her side. He spoke to her of all he was learning about the universe and the tangled threads of lives that intermingled briefly before moving on.

Against all odds, after more than a year, Nina woke up. Her first conscious thought was that she had been asleep and it was morning. She was weak but was used to feeling less than strong. She remembered her courses had come and she had contracted a strange fever that would come and go intermittently, leaving her exhausted. She had fleeting memories of her father sitting at her bedside crying. 'Why would that have been?' she thought.

Nina turned as the door opened and her Nona walked in, staring in surprise before throwing her apron over her face and fleeing the room, calling out to Nina's Papa, 'Signor, Signor it's a miracle, Signorina Nina is awake!!'

'Of course, I'm awake; nothing's unusual about that,' Nina thought before calling out, 'Well good morning to you Nona,' giggling at Nona's strange behaviour. There was a clomping of boots as Eduard burst into the room and Nina gaped at the strange sight of her Papa looking less than calmly elegant. She was shocked to hear how long she had been asleep; more than an entire year had passed.

Days passed and she recovered strength, taking an interest in the scrolls her father had left on her desk. Realising that her natal chart had alerted her father to her pending death, she chastised him for what he had done to keep her with him. She was horrified that he had dabbled in the occult to keep her alive when her allotted time was up. As she recovered, she became firm friends with her new chambermaid Magdalena, La Stregga's adept. They would sit for hours in the garden laughing and chatting about all manner of things. Magdalena brought a beautiful little book she'd made to show Nina. A Grimoire filled with drawings and writings on every plant and herb growing in the garden and in the region of Italy where they lived.

Nina would take it to bed with her, pouring over the little illuminations Magdalena's talented hands had drawn. One evening, her eyes feeling droopy with sleep, she came across a chapter on familiar spirits, which enthralled her. Falling into a deep sleep, she found herself travelling through heavy snow, not in her human skin but in that of a small red fox. Accompanied by a large male fox, she felt tired but exhilarated by the journey.

When she awoke, she remembered this dream had repeated all through the time she had been in a coma. As time passed and the reality of what her father and La Stregga had done set in, she understood more of the threads that were still to unravel, including the eventual death of her friend Magdalena.

After Nina vanished, Eduard was a broken man but Aelish could not resist visiting just one more time. She wanted her daughter she said. Nina had come into her own power, which was not expected. What Aelish had really wanted was a small pin in the shape of a fox; Nina's favourite little piece of jewellery, which, it seemed, had also vanished.

Aelish left and Eduard never set eyes on her again. He woke on the floor in Nina's chamber, wracked with pain and grief, not seeing a small figure that stood in the corner of the room, tears coursing down her face. Before she left, she placed a little fox-shaped pin and a small pile of shells close to his hand. She sensed the power held within that tiny pin.

Chapter 11
Mabon's Approach

She's changing her gown from green to gold
...the harvest is ripening, as the year grows old.
Mabon's first kiss, felt in the air
...as elders ripen in hedgerows fair.
What do you wish for your harvest this year?
Have you laboured long for your fruits to appear?
Let go the old growth, let the leaves fall
...the fruits of your harvest will come when you call.

Now's the time for making preserves from all you've yielded from your garden or from Wildcrafting as you turn the summer's fruits into jams, syrups, pickles and chutneys for winter. Elderberries, blackberries and hawthorn, jam-packed (pardon the pun) with Vitamins for winter ailment's, will soon be ripe enough to harvest. So it's time to think about the fruits that you have harvested this year. How can all the sweetness be preserved, in order for it to be ingested again in your produce as a reminder of all that you have to be grateful for? An extract from Flora's Herbal Grimoire for Mabon.

'It would be so easy to forget life's simplicity with everything that's happened, wouldn't it?' said Flora; a statement more than a question, her hands busy ladling fruit into jars to water bath.

Vanessa mumbled agreement from the pantry, where she was stacking cooling jars of plum jam, the fruits of another season's harvest. Returning to the kitchen for the next load, she paused to look at her sister, thinking how beautiful she was in the first stages of pregnancy. She smiled to herself as she thought of the secret plans laid, without Flora's knowing, for the following week. Flora had insisted she and Cal wait to hand fast until after Sybille and Sam were home safely, but she had not reckoned with the plans and plots afoot to bring the day closer.

'What are you smirking at Nessa? What are you up to? I know that look by now. You're plotting something.'

Vanessa bent over the table and grabbing an already glistening jar of crimson, tomato relish, rubbed at it enthusiastically as if she had spotted a sticky mark from bottling, which gave her a moment to control the giggle that threatened to burst out. Cal's arrival saved the day as she busied herself taking more jars to the pantry. He was in on the plan; really only Flora didn't know she was about to become a married lady.

Cal scooped Flora up in a bear hug, patting her little rounded belly as he put her carefully down, before reaching over to taste some of the relish remains in the pot. 'Mm, tastes great,' he said, washing his hands at the sink. 'You have a gift. Will you marry me?'

'Only if you wash the dishes.'

He winked at Vanessa who hurried to the pantry again to cover her grin. Despite the death of her mother and little acknowledgement of her grief by her father, she was making headway and her greatest source of support were Flo, Cal and Claire.

Sharing the chores and bringing in another harvest was a soothing, if backbreaking, task but Vanessa was fast becoming an enthusiast and was always there to make sure her sister didn't do too much lifting in the more delicate stages of her first trimester.

One by one the others appeared; Beth came with a soft shawl in pastel tones for the baby, Lily with a beautiful faery wind chime and Maeve with a tiny rattle made with silver filigree and filled with crystal beads. Claire brought a set of three little ragdolls made from scraps of Beth's woven fabrics that looked as if made by the Fae.

Max had a deadline for a paper so had excused himself from the evening. Susan and Alex were on their way, bringing a celebratory cake, some sparkling wine and a jar of dill pickles, which Flora had started to crave, much to the amusement of the others who shared space with her.

'What's going on,' said Flora suspiciously, 'I thought we agreed we'd wait for all of this until after Sam, at least, was home?' Laughing as Jamie arrived with a pair of soft leather booties, Alma in tow, carrying a tiny silver bangle.

'We thought we'd make tonight a first baby shower, sis. I've put some veggies in the oven and marinated some tofu and there're fresh salad greens and sundried tomatoes. Oh and some goat cheese from 'les girls',' as she'd fondly dubbed the goats, 'fresh bread and apples; enough for whoever turns up.'

'Thank you Nessa, that's so thoughtful.'

'Well you're not alone now so we can share all the chores and I do love to cook so what better opportunity that to get you to finally sit down and let us take care of you for a change?'

'Too true,' said Maeve. 'What can I do to help Nessa, lay the table?'

'Great, thanks Maeve. I thought it would be nice out in the big dining room; with the sun streaming in today it's lovely and warm.'

'Sure no problem.' She spun around, laughter escaping as Alma and Jamie arrived. 'Trust you two to know when there's food happening.' She hugged them both in apparent joy but spotting the tiny bangle, she sobered. 'Alma?'

'It's all right Mam, I didn't steal it. I'm done with all of that now I understand the need.' She turned to Flora holding the bangle out. 'It's for the wee one Auntie Flo,' she said in a serious tone, 'the little Fae sent it for her to make her change easier…'

Before Alma could continue, Cal stuttered, 'Her? Change? Do you mean our child is a shaper by birth?' He felt Flora take his hand but there was a buzzing in his ears and all other sound faded; the world began to spin sickeningly around.

He was back in the forest, in his Ivor aspect, where he'd lain pronounced dead and where he'd have stayed dead if it weren't for the Lady's intervention after he tried to deflect the arrow from Aelish's bow.

He lay on his back looking up through the canopy of an enormous beech, his bow at his side, watching the Fae as they flitted. One separated from the throng to hover in front of his eyes, moving so fast as to become merely a blur, the tiny being poked him on the forehead, hard enough to bring tears to his eyes. In her hand, she held a delicate filigree, silver bangle.

'A gift from the Lady,' the Fae piped in lilting tones, 'for the one to come who will be a unique blend of yourself and your love.' A sweet, piercing call echoed through the forest and a wren sat singing its heart out on a low branch above his head.

'Flora!'

He returned to the thread as his aspect Ivor receded.

'Yes love I'm here. What happened? Are you okay?' Her eyes were full of concern; his head rested in Alma's lap.

'What the …I…' Cal trailed off confused as his vision cleared and he felt a sharp pain in his forehead. Rubbing it, he winced.

'Show me, are you hurt?' Flora gasped as she saw the blue-black bruise on Cal's forehead. 'How on earth…?'

Cal met Alma's eyes as he shifted his head in her small lap. She smiled sweetly at him. 'See,' she said, indicating the bangle he held in his hand, 'a gift from the Lady.'

He smiled at her as she rubbed gently at his forehead and the pain disappeared. Between them all, they helped him to his feet; Vanessa pushed a chair under him as he tottered unsteadily and Maeve passed him a glass of water that smelt suspiciously of herbs. Flora grinned as he sniffed it dubiously before taking a healthy gulp; his colour returned instantly.

'What happened, Cal?' Flora repeated.

'Well love, it would appear we have a little shaper in your belly who will also be a seer.'

Flora sat down, her hands visibly shaking. 'Oh wow! Will things ever be normal again do you think?'

'Ha!' Maeve exclaimed. 'Please define normal.'

At that moment Susan and Alex arrived and the group gathered around the table as Vanessa and Maeve, with the eager help of Alma, brought out steaming bowls of food.

Jamie stood to invoke a blessing on the food and they linked hands to join in. '*We bless and thank the soil that grows the food we share. May all who eat be filled with strength from this simple fare.*'

Pausing a moment to contemplate the beauty of the food and the sustenance it offered, the quiet was suddenly broken by an all too familiar clatter on the roof. A caw, followed by a loud curse and a thud as something hit the ground hard; then silence. They knew without a doubt who had arrived.

Alma responded by hiding behind Maeve. As Tara walked in, Beth drew herself up to full height ready to demand an explanation as to why she had disappeared when they most needed her. She stopped short from venting her anger when she saw Tara's state. Her clothing was as tattered as ever but dirty and hanging in shreds rather than her usual style of layered, lacy garments. Her once sleek hair was greasy and unkempt but worse was the network of lines running over one side of her face and into her hairline; the streak of white showed more pronounced previously. Worse than her outward appearance was how frail she looked. Always a strong force of nature, she was a shadow of her former self.

'Tara,' cried Maeve, 'what's happened to you?'

Tara made to answer but her face paled even whiter, the lines etched deeper into her skin against the pallor and before she could reply, began to fade in and out.

Claire and Jamie rushed to catch her as she fell, stepping between Flora and Vanessa as they came to help. 'No!' Jamie barked at them, 'don't touch her, especially you Flora. We must keep this blight from your unborn child. Maeve take Alma to the Seer's Isle for safekeeping; speak to The Cybil about Sam.

Nessa do you know if Sam has any of Robyn's elixir left?'

'Yes, I'll get it.'

'Beth, can you find Circaea?'

'Done.'

'Claire, Lily, help me with Tara, we need to take her to Robyn; he'll know what to do.'

'What about Hercurin, wouldn't he help?' Bethan responded quickly.

'No, it's autumn here and he has made his sacrifice to the land. We can't ask more of him at this time as his strength ebbs.'

'Of course,' she replied.

'Flo, do you know where Magdalena's Grimoire is?'

'Yes I have it kept safe for Sam.'

'There may be answers there.'

'Okay I'm on to it.'

'Nessa, did you find Sybille's Book of Shadows among your mother's things?'

'No, not yet. I still have a stack of stuff to go through at the house, but I'll go now.'

'Alex take Susan home, you may not be considered Onceborn but still we don't know the danger of how this is spread.'

Alex nodded curtly, hugged the girls and left rapidly, pulling a protesting Susan behind him.

'Wait,' she called out, 'I can help...' but Alex almost carried her out the door.

Jamie spoke with each of them with staccato speed, authoritatively and without question they responded, their celebration forgotten in the need to act and fast. If it affected a Firstborn, what would be the response from The Morrigan?

Vanessa came back carrying the little vial of elixir, which Jamie administered between Tara's blue-tinged lips.

Tara groaned but remained unconscious as Jamie, Lily and Claire picked her up to take her to Robyn. 'Where are you Pwyll; Morgan?' Claire muttered as they carried Tara through the veil.

'Come on Mam, let's go. The Cybil will help us for sure.' Alma shifted, tugging Maeve behind her.

Cal stood transfixed as everyone scattered to their appointed tasks. 'What about me?' he called after Jamie's retreating figure.

'Look after the girls Cal; help them find Sybille's Book of Shadows. I don't trust to leave them alone. Not even Beth can stand alone against Aelish yet.' With that, he was gone.

Stunned by the turn of events, they cleared away the celebratory food in silence.

'What else can go wrong?' Vanessa groaned. 'Okay Flo, if you look in the Grimoire I'll head over to mum's and take another look around for the Book of Shadows.'

'Let's just hope it's not fallen into the wrong hands and speaking of which,' said Cal, 'we need a safe place to hide this away.' He indicated the tiny bangle in his hand.

'Perhaps with Robyn?' Vanessa suggested.

'No, in the herb bag …it appears to hide things all the time,' said Flo, observing the tiny bird-like Fae as they reappeared on every available surface.

Chapter 12
Vanessa's Search

Dawn in the forest as Her Magicks break free
...hear Her song on the wind that stirs an ancient tree.
In the depths, in the darkness, where all light is dim
...a faint glow can be seen
...at the edge of sight, on the rim.
In your heart you sense Her as she calls, a soft refrain
...in your belly you feel Her; a flutter
...a pang of sweet pain.
As your feet take you walking
...into the depths of Her soft loam
...you'll lay beneath Her fragrant moss
...finding home

 It was hard to walk into her mother's empty house. Already it smelt of mustiness rather than the familiar fragrances of incense or her favourite perfume. Turning the key in the lock Vanessa took a deep breath and walked in, pausing as she heard voices; perhaps she'd left the radio on, she thought.

She was surprised to see Harry's tweed coat on a chair in the hall; she never thought of him as Dad, or even father. Urgent whispers echoing down the near empty hall fell silent as she walked to the back of the house and to her mother's favourite room, a tiny glass fronted conservatory that let in the winter sun. Annie hated winter, which often made Vanessa wonder why her mother had moved to Springsmeet, it had a warm quality even in watery winter sunlight.

Standing still to listen a moment, she then stepped forward quietly to stand in the doorway, the room was ransacked. Harry knelt, dishevelled on the floor, before an open chest usually hidden under a cloth that covered the table Annie had used as a small shrine. She was just in time to see a shadow flit across the room and disappear into the garden; it looked familiar.

Coughing quietly and making her footsteps audible, she walked into the room. Harry snapped round, obviously stressed, a surprised expression on his face at the unexpected interruption.

Before he could speak, Vanessa snapped out 'What are you doing here? You have no right! The will was settled and this is my house and all I have left of my mother.' Holding out her hand, she said, 'Give me the key. They were all supposedly handed to the solicitor when the will was read.'

Harry stood, anger overcoming the surprise of discovery but with a fast recovery said, 'Erm ...I was just looking for some personal letters between your mother and I.'

'Well firstly, you could have asked me and secondly, I can't imagine why you would think they would be in the chest mum used for her Magickal tools, which I'll now take to cleanse, after you've disrespectfully chucked them around. Now, the key please and I'll ask you to leave. If I find anything with your handwriting on it, be assured I'll let you know, until then I don't want to see you here again; in fact I'll be changing the locks immediately.'

This said, she moved to pick up her mother's tools. A lovely, clear quartz-tipped birch wand made her pause. This wasn't her mother's; Maeve had created it for Beth. Puzzled, she turned, almost crashing into Harry, who had moved silently to stand behind her and was looking at the tool intently. Vanessa grabbed a piece of silk and hastily wrapped it, hiding it from his almost greedy gaze. Suddenly he looked different and more than a little crazy-eyed, which made her step back abruptly. As she did, she tripped over an edge of the rug. Falling back heavily against the table edge, she cracked her head on the corner. Harry made no move to help her but only snatched the wand from her nerveless fingers and walked out, throwing his keys on the couch as he passed.

Dazed, Vanessa pulled herself to the closest chair and collapsed in tears. 'What on earth has possessed him?' she cried aloud before passing out.

Vanessa found herself walking a long, pathway through dense forest; a carpet of pine needles and leaves soft beneath her feet. She could see a curl of wood smoke and smell the tang of burning autumn leaves.

Breaking cover from the forest, she was once again in the clearing where Nina's little cottage stood. A tall male figure with silver-streaked, dark hair leant on a garden rake, watching the flames dance in a bonfire. Sprites joined the dance and a small, wizened being sat on a crude bench outside the cottage. She waved to Vanessa as if expecting her and beckoned her over, indicating she sit next to her. Eyes wide, Vanessa observed the strange entity from the corner of her eye before asking, 'Why am I here, Nina's gone?'

Reaching out, Nangini tapped her sharply on the navel, causing her to gasp. 'No, Nina is not gone, she lives on in you and, as your aspect, is always there to share knowledge with you.'

'How do I know what to ask her and how did I get here, come to that?'

'You are here because you dream of this place often and because the Fae, Aerandir would like the opportunity to sit with you and to talk of Nina and of the little light who became a Dark Maker as she fell. He knows more than anyone does, as do you and it is only here that you may speak of what you know. On the thread on which you live there are too many entanglements, whereas here is a clean, bright space that Nina created with the help of a Foxkin. As to what to ask her? Perhaps you are looking for a Grimoire and information to help bring your friends home?'

'I ...no, I was at my mother's cottage looking for Sybille's Book of Shadows but ...' she trailed of hesitantly, 'then I must have hit my head and found myself here. So where is this place in the threads geographically? Flora has the Grimoire, so why would I be looking here?'

Ignoring Vanessa's nervous words, Nangini continued, 'To us this is relative but to you; you will find it close to the ancient Isle of the Seers, hidden in the Mysts. Walk the serpent path and I'm sure you will find it in your realm.'

The tall man turned and Vanessa realised it was the Dark Fae Aerandir. With a rustle of dry leaves, Nangini unfolded cicada-like wings; she stroked Vanessa's cheek. 'You are the light we have waited for and your skills are yet to be unleashed fully. I see you wear the fox pin of your aspect. Wear it well; learn the shifting change and you will uncover your true power. Beware the one who calls you daughter, but know he is not himself,' with that she was gone.

Vanessa blinked rapidly; the air swirled around her full of leaves and giggling leaf sprites. A shadow passed between her and the dappled sunlight as Aerandir stood looking down at her; she'd not heard him approach.

'May I sit?'

'Yes, erm ...of course,' she stuttered, somewhat intimidated by his close proximity.

He looked very different to the sneering Elf Lord she'd met before. He was glowing with a warm light and his dark hair was now predominately silver with a healthy sheen. His once fair skin was no longer pallid and only small tattoos of webbing, remains from the blight, covered a part of his cheek and forehead. Even his clothing was different; gone were the black, thick tunic and hose, replaced by warm autumn tones; his cloak a mantle of leaves and seedpods, which were fragrant with woody blends of oak and nut. He looked remarkably like Aithlin, she thought.

As she scrutinised his changed appearance, she blushed to find he had been observing her with equal interest. For the first time she saw him smile hesitantly, his eyes intense and she felt a surge of attraction as he sat next to her, his hand brushing hers as he did.

'May I call you Nessa?' he asked, his smile broadening.

'Sure,' she returned his smile. 'How are you Aerandir; I may call you that?'

Nodding in affirmation he replied, 'Thanks to our mutual friend, Nina, I am healed of all but the scarring from the blight, which perhaps will fade in time but no matter, it will simply be a reminder of how a Fae can fall from grace and be completely ensorcelled by his own mother.'

'Well, it would appear that she is the mistress of such manipulations; poor little Alma has been a slave to her games it would seem.'

'Ah, yes and there is much more that will be revealed before this game, as you rightly put it, is done.'

'Aerandir, do you know where Sam is?

'Sadly no, but I'm surprised you do not ask of Sybille!' his eyes crinkled at the corners as they narrowed with hidden mirth.

Vanessa grinned in return. 'Well, as you say, there's much to be revealed before the game is up, but for now I must look for Sybille's Book of Shadows. It went missing after she disappeared and perhaps I could look at Nina's version of Magdalena's Grimoire. Flora has a copy on our thread but I have a feeling it may have been altered between threads.'

'It's inside where Nina left it.'

'Really?' Vanessa wanted to dash in and find it but didn't want to appear rude. 'Have you been living here Aerandir? Why haven't you returned to your kin?'

'After the elders chastised me and then, being struck by the blight that Nina healed within me, I have not returned. I also wish to avoid any further contact with Aelish, who in fact I do not believe is my mother, but that is another story and a journey of discovery I shall soon make. Come, I'll show you where the Grimoire is kept.'

They walked to the cottage which, although seemingly the same as when Nina had spent her last days there, was subtly altered by the addition of a few of Aerandir's belongings. A long staff leaned against the wall by the door, a pair of soft, skin boots sat on the hearth and the remains of a meal on the kitchen bench. A small lap harp rested on a chair in the corner by the fire.

'It's beautiful' Vanessa said as she reached out to trace the complex carvings of leaves, flowers and tiny faces peering out from the honey-toned wood.

'A gift from Aithlin.'

'Lucky you, I've wanted to learn and Morgan began teaching me but he too is missing…' she trailed off, her reason for being there returning in sharp focus. 'I need to look for some clues to both Morgan and Sam vanishing but also find a cure for Tara, who seems to have been struck down much as you and Nina were.'

'WHAT?' His demeanour changed instantly and she caught a glimpse of the stern faced Elf she had first seen. When had that been? 'We must act immediately; if the Lady Morrigan knows of this there will be chaos. Has anyone let Aithlin know or Hercurin?' He turned, snatching the little Grimoire from a draw in a small desk. 'Here, take this and I will inform my Uncle of Tara's condition. I suggest you bring her here, Nina's energy remains, especially when you are present, but Flora can help too. She was gifted Airmhid's herbs and the Grimoire secreted within.'

'I think I need to study it here if that's okay. I believe that in the travel between realms, it altered slightly. I don't know how or why but it could be why we have trouble finding the right clues to bring Sybille, Sam and Morgan home and to heal Tara too.'

He took a step closer to her, reaching out tentatively with both hands to encircle her face gently. His hands were warm, surprising her; she'd always seen him as a rather cool being. It made her breath catch in her throat at the intensity of the brief energy exchange. Without asking, he pulled her to him in a hug of friendship but something else lurked below the surface of his calm face; passion and her entire body responded. Alarm bells rang as she thought of all the tales she knew of Fae and human connections. Then again, she thought, a smile of mischief lightening the moment, she wasn't entirely human either. Nessa leant against him, returning his embrace, suddenly feeling a little dizzy and disoriented. The last thing she saw was his face, a look of concern crossing his angled features until she thought she might drown in his liquid, violet eyes.

A sharp rapping sound brought her back to her mother's house. She was sprawled on the floor, Magdalena's Grimoire clutched in her hand; a dull ache clouded her vision as she struggled to rise. Someone was knocking at the front door with obvious urgency and then Cal and Flora burst into the room.

'Nessa!' Flora knelt next to her.

'Here let me.' Cal lifted her onto the couch. 'What happened? You're very pale.'

'I'm not sure …Oh yes, I remember. Harry was here when I arrived; he was rummaging through mum's things. I stood up to him!' She grinned, pleased she'd stood her ground and thrown him out of her house and her life. 'I threw him out but as I started to tidy mum's things I came across the wand Maeve made for Beth. I was holding it and he grabbed it, pushing me over in his rush to leave. Some doctor, eh? Some father, come to that!'

'Oh Nessa-sis, that's dreadful. Let me have a look at you, your pupils are a little dilated and there's a nice bump forming on your head. I'll get you some White Willow bark and arnica ointment; the skin isn't broken …and Cal, could you get an ice pack, please? Where did Annie keep her herbs?'

'There's a cupboard in the kitchen pantry, but I'm fine Flo, really and there's more I have to tell you, but it can wait 'til we're home or at Beth's.'

'Beth's at the shop so we can take you there. I'll get Cal to bring the car round, 'cos we were on foot looking for you. Right now I'm more concerned about you having a concussion, so just wait a moment.' Flora searched her bag, 'Here, a few drops of rescue remedy will help for now but then we need to get you home to bed for a rest; no sleeping though.'

'No Flo, I feel better already and the drops will do the rest. Look, I have the Grimoire too.'

'When did you get back home to get that, this morning?' question Flora, puzzled.

'I didn't, it was at Nina's cottage and Aerandir was there and an odd being made of leaves and twigs ...and ...' she trailed off hesitantly.

Gently Flo hugged her sister. 'Okay, we'll talk it through with Beth and the others. I trust your judgement about your health, but I'm keeping an eye on you and you're not to work today.'

Cal returned with a wrapped ice pack, which he placed gently on the growing bruise on Vanessa's temple. 'Ouch,' he said sympathetically, 'I'll get the car Flo,' and was gone.

Flora and Vanessa sat in silence as the little house seemed to move and shift around them. A flutter of birds on the roof grew louder as the little Fae came down the chimney, settling on every available surface, their eyes taking in everything. They morphed and changed to their Fae form, finishing what Vanessa had started, clearing Annie's tools away and whispering words of cleansing as they carefully wrapped each item before placing them back in her tool chest.

'Thank you,' Vanessa said quietly, feeling suddenly tired but she was no longer afraid of who she was and there was work to do; Cal arrived to take them home.

Chapter 13
Alma

Sweet dreams, disturbed by a sound
…you can hear if you listen, there's anger and pain
…rhythms: a heartbeat, ear close to the ground
…the Lady stirs, shards break when used for ill gain

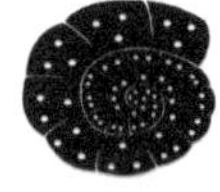Alma loved the shop, it was full of wonderful objects that spoke to her and now that they didn't whisper, 'Steal me, make people suffer loss as you have suffered,' she had the time to listen to their music.

She cleaned, polished and blessed each item and the sales of such things skyrocketed overnight. To all that came and went she was a little shadow, caught on peripheral when they least expected; spoken of in hushed tones …'I'm sure I saw a quaint little being with long, snarled hair and huge, green eyes,' said one visitor in a whisper.

'I think you may have a ghost,' said another regular, 'I keep seeing this bedraggled, waif of a child.'

'Oh no,' they would reply, 'that's just Alma; she's Maeve's …erm, ward.' Alma took pleasure at the thought of people speaking of her in hushed tones.

Weeks passed in the lineal time of the earth realms and Alma grew. Now at twelve winters, she was as slender as a reed, never forgetting her experiences but not letting them rule her with anger or pain. She'd not only grown physically but also matured. Boys passing her in the street saw a rather feral but very pretty girl, with her small features, wild curling mane of titian red hair, long legs and extraordinarily huge eyes. They wondered who she was and why she didn't attend school. One bold lad even knocked on the door of 'earthly rites,' having followed Maeve and Alma home one day.

'She's home schooled,' was Maeve's stern reply, 'and she doesn't speak English,' at which Alma giggled aloud.

After a while, she became the mystery of Springsmeet and Covenstead, furthering the fast growing stories Sybille's continued absence engendered and also that no one had seen Morgan or Sam around recently. Of course, there were always the gossips who preferred the story she was Maeve's child, '…and her still single,' they whispered.

Sybille had always fascinated the Onceborn and now her group of 'acolytes' were fuel for the rumourmongers. 'Small towns, no matter how busy, always have the gossips and taletellers,' Maeve thought to herself as she worked.

She'd kept hidden the beautiful tools Cal and Maeve had made and occasionally heard them singing to her; she hoped Lady Aelish couldn't. Pausing, she realised she could only hear the snood but not the wand and felt herself go still and cold inside. Surely her hiding place had been safer than any other, deeper than the Lady's Chalice well itself.

Feeling a strange sense of panic she dropped her cleaning cloths and ran to find Bethy, she would know what to do. 'I promised,' she began to sob. 'I promised Lady Arianwen I would look after them. What if …oh no,' she groaned. 'What if *she's* got it?'

Beth wasn't around and her panic grew to fear; where was everyone. Suddenly the lovely old house was full of whispers and scratching sounds.

It took a lot to scare her but suddenly she was scared. Fighting what she knew to be illusion she stopped still in her initial rush of panic to find Beth and the house stilled again. Clammy with cold sweat and the fear that nibbled at her guts, Alma sat on the bottom step of the stairs that led to Flo's herb room. She knew Flo had a client so she couldn't just barge in there.

Vanessa had guests at reception so she couldn't go there either and Mam was out somewhere getting supplies for her work. Cal was at home, Claire too; they were studying the scratchy script. Bird cuneiforms, Cal had called them. Sam was gone, Morgan too; she whispered to herself where everyone was like a litany; suddenly she felt so alone.

Her sight began to blur, she hadn't been sick since the time her first blood had come, on another thread in the weave. Now she saw her reflection in the glass door, opposite where she sat and she looked just like the ghost people described seeing. Steadying her hands by clasping them tightly together, she began to chant a little invocation to her water spirit kin.

'*I have need of your aid …hear me call, come to me. Water spirits stop your play; call our kin, come to me. I am afraid and alone and the world has gone dark. Here me call sister kin …stop your play this is no lark.*'

Alma rocked as she sang but she could hear the water pipes in the old house begin to bubble and way up in the attic in Maeve's studio she knew the cauldron was beginning to boil. Just the sound of her water friend's reply to her call was enough to calm her. Leaning her head against the stair rail, she quietened her breathing until the house became still and the miasma over her eyes cleared.

She remembered when Beth had spoken with her about the treasures she'd hidden in her secret place; the importance of that moment was finding Sam's bracelet…

'*I am Arianwen,*' she'd said, '*this silver bracelet was lost and I have searched for it. I thank you for looking after it so well that it can be returned to its rightful owner.*'

Alma nodded. '*S'al'rite,*' she whispered shyly, watching with huge mooneyes as the beautiful lady floated through the chamber towards where she sat, surrounded by her stash of jewellery, shells and stones piled in the centre of the earthen floor.

'*What else have you here, little one?*' Arianwen asked her kindly. Alma knew she'd already spotted the mesh snood Maeve had made for her; Alma had thrown it away from her when it hurt her head so much and the wand

Cal had created, but she'd merely smiled at Alma and hadn't been cross with her like M'lady always was.

Pointing to the lovely things, Beth had merely said, *'Keep those pieces very safe won't you. Don't let anyone know you have them, will you. I entrust them into your keeping until the time I shall ask you to return them to me. Then will you do so; will you promise me?'*

'Yer, promise,' Alma whispered.

'Good, then we're friends and I'll look after you, little one. You may come with me if you will. It will be a very different life, but we will care for you. Don't you want to see Maeve again?'

Alma would never forget her kindness and now, exactly what she'd promised Beth wouldn't happen had; the precious wand was missing.

Chapter 14
Beth and Alma

Daylight is fading …winter draws in
…cold winds are blowing…ice on your skin.
Slowly as leaves fall …golden light fades
Dreams of snow falling …in quiet loamy glades
…weaving the magic in silent moonlight
…softly He comes in the frost of dawn's light
A blanket of cover …like sparks on the earth
Listen carefully; you'll hear Him
…with His deep-bellied mirth.

Strangely, when Maeve had tried to reach the Isle with Alma, she was blocked and Alma had merely looked at her with wise and ancient eyes. 'We'll have to go back Mam. Beth will be able to come through with me but for some reason The Cybil won't let you back.'

So now Beth and Alma travelled the roads between without apparent haste and yet the journey was over in a flash as they stood on the jetty looking toward the Seer's Isle, hidden in the Myst.

Embarking in the coracle that waited, they travelled through the damp, early morning to the Isle. On arrival, Beth realised that even Oonah hadn't put in an appearance. An eerie stillness hung over everything, there wasn't even the smell of wood smoke, usually so redolent in the air.

Climbing from the coracle and up the steps from the jetty, Alma appeared nervous, her eyes scanning everything as she peered through the Myst.

Nothing, there was nothing. No sounds or familiar smells and no sign of movement, no settlement sat hugging the shoreline with its back to the trees. No laughter rang; no bells tolled, the Seer's village had vanished without a trace.

'What in the name of ...' Beth halted, stunned as Leah stirred within her. 'What happened?' she asked Leah directly. 'It's as if it were never here. Where's Sybille? Where are all the priestesses and adepts?'

'This is not the thread you sought Arianwen,' Leah replied in her mind. 'This is a moment that is but a potential, which will only occur if the day comes when all forget the Isle of Seers. Had this happened we would not be conversing, for I will not have existed and all the events to date would be but dreams,'

'Then how do we protect the Seer's Isle?'

'It will, as it must, disappear into the Skeins of Tyme, where only a few will remember the way back to Her. On your thread, already there is a return to the Old Ways but tainted with ego and pride as those who seek power over others, claim knowledge of which they have no idea. It is a game of power over, rather than power to and this in turn is more dangerous than any truth may be.

The Cybil will be on another thread teaching those who will listen to the truth of the Old Ways and Sybille, her aspect was doing the same until she vanished.'

'Do you know where she is and how we can speak with The Cybil, Leah?'

'It would appear that The Cybil does not wish to speak with you right now Lady,' and with that, Leah fell into silence.

Alma stood shivering as she looked around her. Her hand snuck into Beth's seeking comfort.

'I can barely remember this thread, Bethy, although somehow I know I was here,' she whispered, close to tears. 'Why does the Lady hide the truths we ask? Why is it so hard to make sense of the Song?' To which Beth had no reply. Inside though she felt like shaking her fist at the illusive Goddess who hid truths in unforseen places and made Her followers work to earn Her favour. 'Frankly,' she thought, 'I'm exhausted by it all.'

From deep in the forest birds began stirring, their trilling songs rang through the crisp morning air and a drum began throbbing the sunrise. Figures, misty and vague, stood along the forest rim. They were half-naked, painted with blue woad spirals and swirls, battle ready. One arrow snaked its way through the sky to land at Beth's feet. Its flight quill was a blue-black raven feather, its owner a tall, slender female; tattoos covered much of her arms, upper torso and one side of her face. Beth knew she was a Firstborn of the Raven Goddess, The Morrigan.

With a nod and a ghost of a smile, the female merged back into the forest behind her with her kin. A large male of impressive stature saluted her and Tara's familiar silver streaked wings flashed and dipped in greeting in the sunlight; her laughter echoed.

Alma's giggle of pure delight brought Beth back to herself.

'What does it mean, Alma?'

'Lady, you know if you look we are but on a thread, long ago in Tyme when the Firstborn walked the land, born of the Raven Goddess. Free and unfettered by humankin's interference or Dark Fae manipulations come to that. Come on Lady, let's go back to the others and tell them that Sam, Morgan and Tara are safe and will find their own way back through the roads Between just at the right moment.'

'Okay, stay here a moment Alma, I need to see if there is any trace of the settlement so that we can gauge at what time the Priestesses lived here on the Isle. I can't sense Leah at all so I imagine this is, as you say, a thread long before any other.' With that, she wandered off to the edge of the forest.

Despite Beth asking her to wait, Alma wrapped herself in a soft wool cloak, given to her by Bethan for the journey and slipped silently away, a shadow in the night as a waning moon, at its last slender sliver, rose in the sky.

Perhaps, she thought, after seeing the Firstborn in the forest, she could find them; speak with them about Aelish.

Walking through the trees to the edge of the lake she remembered how she'd behaved; missing an opportunity to become a seer, a priestess for the Isle of Mysts because of her obnoxious behaviour. Influences beyond her control had fashioned her the way she was and the tangled threads of her small tapestry had suddenly stretched and warped until she no longer knew the truth of herself. She now did and, as she'd said only recently to her friends and parents, knowing who you were just in this moment had to be enough.

Now she needed to find Aelish and help find the chink in the armour that would let them heal the trail of grief created by one small Dark Fae. 'Who were Aelish's parents?' Alma wondered. 'They couldn't conceivably be the Forest Fae clan that Aithlin belonged to; was she even truly his sister?' She thought not; Aerandir was proving to be an ally thanks to Nina's compassion.

Deep in the watery depths a lonely creature stirred, hearing the call to wake. Merrow and Water Sprites, dancing on the surface, called to Alma as Beth returned to collect her.

'Listen Lady,' Alma whispered, 'the Sprites and Merrow have something to tell you.'

Straining to listen to the high watery tones, all Beth could hear was, 'A'maelamin tinu. Amin ilyanemie utu lle imya llie Lindale.' 'Daughter, my beloved daughter, I will always find you through your song.'

Beth's sight blurred as she remembered the first time her father Aithlin had said the very same words to her when he first revealed himself to her. 'Who …is that? Who are you; do you mock me?'

Alma took her hand gently, her grin wide and filled with joy. 'Shhh,' she said, finger to lips, 'no one must know yet Lady'; she whispered a name in Beth's ear and tears welled.

Chapter 15
Whom to Trust?

Once again, despite Flora's concerns for her sister's wellbeing, the group travelled the threads Between Tyme to Robyn's home on the outskirts of Glastonbury.

One by one they appeared from all directions. From the chill of an autumn evening to the chill of a fresh spring day, the group emerged at the designated time, entering through the portal of Susan's painting, where Aerandir and Aithlin joined them. Aerandir carried Tara, as he believed he would be immune now to the blight that had struck the shaper down. No one knew what to say, in light of Tara's condition, which seemed to be worsening.

Robyn had food ready for their arrival but no one was hungry, concern for Tara etched in their nervous, strained faces. He handed each of them a chilled glass of spring tonic, made of strawberries and wild herbs collected in the early dawn of the day at Chalice Well. The red tinged waters from the well coloured the clear sparkling water from his farm spring.

Tara had not stirred since Aerandir laid her on the couch Robyn had indicated. She was paler than ever and the dark, twisted webbing stood out in relief against her pallor. 'Does the Raven Mother know of this?' Robyn questioned Beth.

'We haven't heard anything yet but I'm sure she would automatically be aware of any harm to her Firstborn.'

'True, but the Morrigan is a strangely unpredictable Goddess,' Robyn replied with a grimace. 'Well, no time for that now, did Flo bring the book and Nessa the Grimoire?'

'Yes and Nessa has a story to tell from earlier today.'

On hearing Nessa's name, Aerandir straightened from where he was tending to Tara. 'She collected it from the cottage this afternoon, believing the copy was altered by the changed threads, but I fear the same may occur when she brought it back here. She was about to ask me if I minded her staying to study it, which of course I didn't, but she suddenly disappeared. Is she all right?'

'Yes, she's here Aerandir,' Beth said, indicating to where Vanessa stood quietly observing, as was her way.

With a final stroke of Tara's hair, he walked across to Vanessa. 'Are you all right, you disappeared so quickly I was concerned?'

'Yes, I'll share the story with everyone shortly, rather than repeating it again but thank you for your concern.' Aerandir thought he would drown in her liquid brown eyes; he recalled Nina's pools of grief and wanted to hold her again.

'I never said to you how sorry I am for your mother's death. If you ever need to …' Robyn cut him off, calling them all to sit. Vanessa squeezed his hand in thanks.

'I understand Nessa has something to share from her day with us, which appears to add another player in the game under the influence of Aelish.

'How did you …? Ah, never mind, I know! You have ears and eyes everywhere,' she grinned but there was an air of concern about the statement. Nessa told the story of the morning's incidents, leaving out nothing, even her encounter with Aerandir; her eyes warming as their eyes met.

Robyn cleared his throat, bringing them both back to the moment, but it was clear for all to see what was happening between them. Susan sighed, 'Oh no, not another changeling match,' she whispered to Alex.

'Well, we have a daughter who has changer ancestry somewhere so it's not for us to comment.' Susan bit back a reply as she saw Beth watching, one eyebrow raised questioningly.

'Would you say the same then for Flo and Cal, Susan?' Claire interjected.

'No …I just …I just mean it makes everything so complicated for them.'

Aerandir stood to speak, bringing their attention back to the meeting.

He cleared his throat, 'I have been trying to remember something. It's about Aelish and the letter that was left for you Uncle, when Minhiriath died,' he nodded respectfully to Aithlin. 'Do you still have it?'

'Yes, of course, but why?'

'Could you fetch it?'

'Erm …no need I …' he pause, seemingly embarrassed; his pale cheeks flushed red as he rummaged in his tunic pocket next to his heart. 'I have it with me always.' He handed it to Aerandir reluctantly. 'Have a care with it lad, it's old and precious to me, despite the circumstances.'

Aerandir carefully opened the crumpled, fading note; the ink was strangely sepia toned and a shiver went through him as he realised it was blood. He translating from Elvish as he read aloud…

'Aithlin, I cannot continue, something is wrong and my body is weak; my mind fades. I want you to take our children to Susan and Alex and place them in their care. I know you won't take them back to your tribe as changelings they will be, but I ask that you keep an eye on them carefully. Do this

for me, for us …for your children …don't grieve me, for I will go home …' the writing trailed off abruptly.

Exchanging glances with Susan and Alex, Beth approached Aerandir. 'Let me see; are you translating this correctly.'

'Of course, Arianwen. Why would I not? I believe this concerns me as much as it does you. Lady, I have seen the evil done that day …I scried …and saw. Sarah may have written the note, but more happened before she became so weak; yet more after she lapsed unconscious and your father was in no state to take in the details. Elven is a difficult language to translate accurately and words such as child and children are too close to distinguish without full knowledge about what the person was trying to say.'

Claire spoke up. 'There was more than one child! Is that what *you're* trying to say Aerandir?'

'Yes, it is.' Turning to Aithlin he said, 'We cannot blame you, you were in a terrible state and you have long since apologised to Arianwen for not contacting her sooner to let her know of her ancestry but I would ask one thing of you. Search back in your memory to that evening and who else was around at the lake, close by.'

'You ask much of me lad, I have been back repeatedly in my mind until I cannot look any more. I am, even after all these years, only partially recovered from the loss of Sarah …Minhiriath. I will mourn her always.'

At that moment, Alma appeared from nowhere.

'We told you to stay with The Cybil,' said Maeve sternly.

'I'm not being naughty Mam but Aerandir contacted me through the water sprites asking I come to back up what he may have discovered.'

'But you weren't even born then!' Maeve insisted, running her hands through her hair in frustration. 'I don't think I'll ever get used to all the twists and turns in the threads.'

'I may not have been born in the way you mean Mam but I was around; I knew Minhiriath. I met her in the deep when Aelish took me; changed me to suit her needs. You tried to rescue me, Mam,' she said hearing Maeve's sharp intake of breath.

Silence fell at her words. Beth came to kneel in front of the strange little child. 'Tell us what you know; both of you,' she turned to Aerandir. 'Tell us now.'

'We need Aithlin to remember, Bethy,' Alma said gravely. 'There was someone else there on that evening that he has forgotten. Grief will do that I know.'

Robyn approached Aithlin. 'Come Aithlin, let me help you. Sit here and I will take you back to that evening. We will all witness what you have to say and then, if you will, I shall erase the pain of remembering.'

'Nothing can be worse than what I already know, surely.'

'May the Goddess make it so,' murmured Aerandir.

Leading him to a comfortable chair, Robyn administered a large dose from a vial of silvery liquid; the substance appeared filled with cobweb threads.

Aithlin quickly fell into a restless hypnotic state as he listened to Robyn's voice, guiding him back to the moments he would never forget. After a while, he began to speak, haltingly at first, his voice strengthening as he connected with the thread.

'I went searching for Sarah as night fell, at Susan's promptings, although I thought, because of the rain, Sarah was just enjoying the wild energy of nature she so loved. A storm rose from nowhere and I could barely see but I went to her favourite spot on the lake in Springsmeet and there I found her body. One tiny girl child lay close to her, barely breathing. I administered a drop of elixir and the little one stirred, opening curious, violet eyes, older than any newborn child's eyes should be.

Next to Sarah's body was a note, weighted with a stone,' he indicated to the tattered page Aerandir still held, 'as if she had pre-thought her death but we know no Fae would ever take their own life and a Water Merrow could not drown unless their gills were sealed shut, against either air or water.

I held her, assuming by her inertia that her spirit had fled; I was unaware of the ability a Water Spirit has to put themselves into a deep trancelike state when attacked but she was deathly still.

I knew the ways of her tribe; beside myself with grief, I placed Minhiriath back into the lake for her kin to bear home. I saw her familiar, Oonah come to take her home. I watched as she towed my loves' body away from me forever.

I read that note repeatedly but only now I realise what Aerandir has seen. She wrote children, not child and yet there was only a little girl left behind.'

Aithlin's voice faltered as his eyelids flickered in rapid recall; he gasped, tears coursed down his cheeks unchecked. 'Yessss,' he hissed, 'I see someone now, standing on the other side of the lake, holding something in their arms. It's moving, struggling and I can hear a feeble cry but then Beth cries too and I know I must get her to Susan and Alex as soon as possible and oh Goddess, I forgot what I'd seen in my selfish grief.'

'Look deeper,' Robyn intoned in a deep, clear voice. 'You're not alone, we are all with you; we can all see through your eyes as you speak. Look deeper into the shadows where the other stands. Who is it and what are they holding?'

The answer came, Aithlin's voice raw with tears and rage, 'It's Aelish and she is holding another baby. I sense it's a boy.' He stumbled over his words again. 'At that time my sister Aelish was pregnant, we believed with a Fae whom we didn't know. She was vain, stupidly so, but I always thought she was too slender for the good of the child she carried but of course there was no child of hers.

I see now as she stands there gloating, having killed my love. She took my child. She stole OUR child and called him hers. Oh Minhiriath, what did she do to you? Why would my own sister do such a thing to ME?'

Abruptly Aithlin ripped back into his conscious body; pain and grief wracked his face. His eyes opened wide as he pointed at Aerandir, his face paradoxically changed to joy in a second. 'You're not Aelish's son; you're ours; Sarah's and mine. …You're Arianwen's twin brother.'

A stunned and awkward silence fell before everyone spoke at once. Beth, tears in her eyes, reeling with shock, approached her father and her brother where they stood locked in a hug of joy mixed with sorrow for the lost years of unknowing.

As she approached, they broke apart but only to include her in their sheer delight. Sorrow put aside for a while, they expressed their feelings openly with everyone, which was unusual for Faefolk.

Beth knew intuitively her mother's presumed death was exactly how Aelish had wanted it to appear to everyone. With Minhiriath gone there was no one to see through her machinations and perhaps, finally, Aelish would discover her own parentage. She was convinced Aelish was not Aithlin's sister as was told.

A small voice spoke up, breaking into Beth's thoughts and putting a halt to the laughter and chatter.

'Lord Aithlin, she's not dead.' Alma glanced at Beth questioningly; she nodded imperceptibly.

'Minhiriath was not dead when you found her but close to it; so close it would be impossible, even for you, to tell the difference. She'd slipped into her deeper state and into her Otter friend Oonah. She had only moments before her physical body would cease to be animated by her Fae Spirit but too late. Aelish sealed her gills with mud; her body drowned only moments after you Aithlin, slid her body back into the lake, believing her already beyond help. You saw Oonah tow Minhiriath's body through the Between, to the Lake of Mysts. Water Spirits and Sprites tended her body and they managed to restore a semblance of life in which her Spirit still resides. Just as humans lose brain cells when starved of air, so too do the Water Spirits when starved of water or air for too long. Minhiriath has lived a half-life in the waters of the sacred lake, she has never spoken again; she is always sad and bereft for something she's trying to remember. She is only completely conscious when she shares her familiar spirit's body,'

'Much as Rowan and Ruark?' Cal interjected.

Eyes downcast, Alma fell silent, gauging how much more she could say. When no one said anything, she continued quietly, 'She's changed recently. Something is bringing her back. She's trying to speak and calling for you. The Cybil sent me to tell you.'

'What!' Aerandir could hardly contain his rage, once more looking like the Dark Fae he had become through Aelish's influences. 'The Cybil has known this and has never thought it fit to share that information!'

Beth reached out but he shook her off; Maeve stepped between Alma and him. 'Don't even think about it Aerandir.' Jamie moved forward in the midst of change, teeth bared at the Fae. 'Don't shoot the messenger either; she's doing what she was instructed to do. Don't make me regret trusting you ELF!'

At that moment, Lily and Max stepped through the veil. Not knowing what had transpired, they immediately moved to protect Alma from the perceived threat.

Alma quietly moved around them all taking Aerandir's hand in hers. 'I know what you're feeling. I have felt it all, never knowing where you came from or what you are in truth. Anger got me nowhere and now, knowing at least who my parents are on one thread is enough. Everything else, all the twisty-turns in the threads, are nothing to knowing that. Now we have work to do to find Sam, Morgan and Sybille. Are you with us Aerandir?'

He smiled at the childlike innocence of the little being who knew so much and who held so many secrets locked in her consciousness. He wondered what she really was.

Her words had an immediate effect on everyone but Aerandir stood, staring at Robyn, wise enough to know that his relationship with The Cybil and also her aspect

Sybille had a role to play in the scheme of things. His eyes said, 'Another time Old One; enough for now but I'm not done with you yet.'

Maeve pulled Alma aside. 'I know you went with Beth after you couldn't get through the Myst with me but how many other times have you slipped away to see The Cybil?'

Head down, fingers crossed behind her back, Alma replied airily, 'Oh not often Mam.'

A hush fell again as Robyn, Susan and Alex told their perspective of the night of Minhiriath's death.

Chapter 16
Minhiriath; Sarah 29 years ago

Can you dream
...or does illusion bind you your wings?
As watery depths enfold you, coldness stings
...can you dream?

Sarah Lyndon was a rather secretive person, rarely trusting anyone with the truth of her ancestry. While she, enjoyed the humankin and their somewhat naïve lives, she was a creature of water and her Trueshaper name was Minhiriath (meaning between the rivers) Isil'Lindir, in the Fae language.

Her mother, Circaea Isil'Lindir, had been pleased when her daughter found a balance between her dreams of a human life and her ancestry. Minhiriath, fascinated to learn about the shaper cells that must be present in the human strain through interspecies breeding, found her calling studying anthropology and that of human genes.

Susan Fenner had been the instigator for Sarah, as she called herself in the human realm, to study the world of man, to educate the Fae and in turn, their kin. Building much needed bridges, she said, so that the Fae could return to live side by side with their humankin. All were interconnected and it was not right that such a divide had grown between them when they were originally of the same blood and of the Mother.

Sarah was convinced that the keys to healing many human diseases was hidden in the blood of their ancestral Fae kin but there were few Fae who would step forward to help her research these theories, except one, who clearly understood her endeavours. His name was Aithlin Farandir and he was just the Fae to help hold the balance between the worlds too.

To Circaea's delight, he and Minhiriath fell deeply in love, crossing boundaries so that one of water and one of the earth and forests could unite.

Tragedy struck both the Fae and human realms when Minhiriath was almost full term with their child. Minhiriath had said to Aithlin that she would stay the night with Susan and Alex Fenner. Their little boy Max was a delight and she loved to spend time with the little family, dreaming of the day that her own little one would play with Max, now just two years old. They often spoke of their children becoming fast friends and how the closeness, between human and Fae realms would enrich their lives.

Aithlin would hold back from interaction with her friends; he was of the forests and urban life was not to his liking. Instead Susan, Alex and little Max would join them at Covenstead. At Sybille's home in the hills and Aithlin could relax, playing for them and speaking in depth of his people.

On one such weekend when they were staying at Sybille's, Minhiriath wandered off saying she needed to be in the water again. As her time drew near, she went more and more to the lake in Springsmeet, drawn to the waters that were clean and clear; minerals were rich in their cold depths. She would travel through the underground springs to bathe and renew her watery self. She was a Water Spirit and the little cousins, Sprites and Merrow, were always there waiting when she came to bathe and play.

Night fell and still she had not returned. Sarah and Alex had taken Max back to their home in Melbourne and Sybille sat in the cool evening air with Aithlin, listening to the growing night-songs and watching the leaf sprites play.

Sybille thought of her friend Robyn and spoke to Aithlin about a trip to the UK she had planned for Beltane. She kept talking, sensing Aithlin's growing restlessness as Minhiriath still didn't return, until he stood abruptly and wished her a pleasant night, saying he had to find Sarah; concerned for her wellbeing and then he was gone.

Sybille searched the aethers for a sign of Sarah but found no trace. Calling on her friend Tara, she waited, tension mounting, knowing something was not right.

Aithlin didn't return and Tara hadn't responded to her friend's call either. Sybille rang Susan and Alex to see if Sarah had returned there but they were none the wiser.

'Do you want us to come back, Sybille?' Susan asked.

'No, I'll keep you posted if I hear anything.'

'Well, you know how erratic Sarah can be, so don't worry too much just yet. I'm sure Aithlin will find her if any one can.'

Night fell and a storm rose from nowhere. On the banks of Springsmeet Lake Aithlin found his lover's body. One tiny girl child lay close to her, barely breathing. He administered a drop of elixir and she stirred, opening curious, violet eyes that were older than any newborn child's should be.

Next to her body was a note weighted with a stone as if she had pre-thought her death, but no Fae would ever take her or his own life and a Water Merrow could not drown unless their gills were sealed shut against either air or water.

Aithlin held Minhiriath to his chest, assuming by her inertia that her spirit had fled, unaware of the Water Spirits ability to put themselves into a deep trancelike state when attacked.

Knowing the ways of her tribe, wracked with grief, he placed Minhiriath back into the lake for her kin to bear home. Minhiriath, not dead but close to it, slipped into her deeper state and into her Otter friend Oonah. She had only moments before her physical body would cease to be animated by her Fae Spirit but too late, with her gills sealed her body drowned only moments after Aithlin slipped her body back into the lake, believing her already beyond help.

Oonah towed Minhiriath's body through the Between to the Lake of Mysts. Water Spirits and Sprites tended her body, managing to restore a semblance of life in which her Spirit could reside. Just as humans lose brain cells when starved of air so too do the Water Spirits when starved of water or air for too long. Minhiriath lived a half-life in the waters of the sacred lake, never speaking again, sad and bereft for she knew not what.

What Aithlin failed to see on the evening he found Minhiriath's body and his child was a dark slender Fae standing across the lake observing him coldly. In her arms, she held a boy child whose face was the perfect replica of his father and his twin sister.

Minhiriath's note stated that her 'children' be sent to Susan and Alex as she knew Aithlin would not take them back to his tribe. He was in no state to query the word 'children,' rather than 'child' and it made no mention of her mother or her own Watery kin.

In his grief, he did exactly what her note had told him to do and he felt no emotion then for the tiny scrap of life which was his daughter. He slipped between the realms, leaving the little girl at Susan and Alex's with the will Sarah had drawn up should she die before Bethan was grown. To them it seemed that he left without a backward glance. They did not see him again until his reappearance after Beth turned twenty-nine.

Grief does strange things to the psyche and so Susan and Alex raised the little girl as their own, although they told her about her mother, leaving out her otherworldly existence until Arianrhod, at Silver's behest, commanded Aithlin tell his daughter of her ancestry.

Max, when presented with a new sibling and pre-cocious at three, asked his mother why she hadn't had a big belly like his friend's mummy. He adored his little sister, their closeness persisted through adolescence and into adulthood; they looked out for each other.

Bethan grew into a resilient, gentle child. Susan and Alex often wondered where Aithlin had gone and if one day he would change his mind and come for her.

Beth never caused them a moment of grief, having the innate ability to reason with her parents when she wanted something for which they weren't sure she was ready. They were thrilled when she graduated school and headed for Uni to study, as Susan had, fine art and tex-tiles. Like magnets, the daughters of Susan and Claire were drawn together to become life-long friends.

Aithlin drew away from all but the Elders of his tribe, vanishing into the Between to heal his wounds. His guilt at being unable to protect his love, let alone prevent her death, ate away at him to the point that he could not look at his daughter or be near her until she was more than old enough to understand and only then had he acted forced by Silver's insistence. Now Aithlin had not only a daugh-ter but also a son, her twin.

Chapter 17
Lost Souls

Watery depths of oceans and lake
...calling your innermost soul to awake
Float in her darkness both salty and sweet
...ride on her waves to the shores of deep sleep
Life is her gift, through the blood in your veins
...the lymph that flows gently as it pools and drains
Through every cell and under your skin
...swim in her depths...find your tail, grow a fin
In her dark pools seek; find your watery kin

Deep in the Lake of Mysts a creature stirred, hearing the song lost long ago to her. It swelled and then began again, a deeper note intervening and yet each was a replica of the other.

As they are constantly immersed in water, Water Spirits and Sprites do not cry, for that would be a contradiction and yet there was a remembering that moved through what was left of the creature's sanity.

It was a subtle yet haunting memory of physical pain, sudden mewling cries and the sense of tiny beings lying on her breast as she struggled to reach the lake to take them home to their watery kin. Then there had come pain as one of them was ripped away from her during the birth process itself; the other cried shrilly in distress for her womb brother. Pain wracked her, the pain of her gills glued shut by a cloying mass of black ichor that burned her tender skin, before darkness was all there was behind her eyes.

She recalled a voice calling to her to come back, but she could not respond, though she lay in the strong familiar arms of her lover. These thoughts would come and go as she drifted, lured by the sounds of music from above the surface of the lake and yet she knew this was a different thread and indeed a different lake to where she had experienced the pain of birth, loss and what may as well have been her death.

A small Merrow visited her often, a strange wild creature, who had known much pain. She had screamed in pain and rage when the sprites had brought her back to the lake after being born as a child, a seer with potential for the Isle of the Seers. Rage for the life, cut short; she knew who the cause of both their pain was.

Minhiriath understood all that the strange spirit said but could not answer; she was locked in her own world of grief and pain, until finally the Merrow disappeared and she was again alone.

Threads merged with threads, lives; aspects intermingled until there was only a deep longing left to her; for what she could not remember. On occasion there would come a fleeting memory of tiny, soft creatures. They cried in anger; released from a warm, watery womb into the cold world. She had no idea they were the children she'd never actually met. At other times she heard a rich male voice calling out. Sometimes he sat on the edge of the lake and cried bitter tears of loss; she wondered for whom his tears fell.

Tonight, in answer to Beth's call, Circaea sat with her granddaughter and grandson, on the edge of the lake, communing with the Water Spirit who struggled to remember who she was. Oonah swam frantically in circles and Leah stirred in response.

'We have work to do together Leah,' Beth called out with her mind. Aerandir reached out to take her hand. 'We'll get her to the elders Arianwen,' he no longer called her Beth. 'They will help her heal and perhaps you and I will have a mother.'

'It's hard for me to imagine. I've been very blessed with Susan and Alex as my parents, Max as my brother and they will always remain so. This is different; she is the mother of my body and yours, daughter to our grandmother Circaea. Yes, we will bring her home.'

Chapter 18
The Grimoire

All that you say is heard by the birds
...have a care, believe me they hear every word.
All of your thoughts and all of your dreams
...for birds are not really, all they seem.
They're the Lady's little Magicks, the Fae in disguise.
Look closely you'll notice, it's hidden deep in their eyes.

 Vanessa and Flora sat at the huge table in the dining room, both Grimoire open in front of them. At first glance they appeared to be identical, but closer inspection showed the copy Vanessa had brought back was covered with minute notes in an unknown script. It was recognisable as Elvish but strange markings encircled the text.

'It looks as if the birds have been walking all over it,' said Flora. 'We'll need a magnifying glass to see clearly but I don't have a clue what these scratching's mean.'

'There's a pattern to them though, look Flo,' Vanessa pointed to a group of cyphers. 'They almost look like there's a rhythm, a pattern to them like musical notes. I wish Morgan were here or Pwyll but perhaps Aerandir will help.'

'Perhaps but can you go back to the cottage or was that a fluke do you think?'

'I'm not sure I'd find the way Flo, but if we could contact Jamie he would take me there for sure. Perhaps I could even practice shifting.'

'What? You're a shaper too? When did that happen?'

'Well, it hasn't yet.' Vanessa backtracked quickly, realising she had almost revealed one of the secrets held in reserve.

Flora looked at her suspiciously, not easily fooled. 'Okay, whenever you're ready to talk about it, but I'm really tired of all the secrecy, it's getting us nowhere.'

Vanessa hated lying by omission to her sister but it was so easy to slip up. Excited by the prospect of discovering what Jamie had taught Nina, and now that she had the fox head pin, she couldn't wait to find out for herself.

They continued studying the old text and the strange markings on the pages. Suddenly Vanessa paused, reaching for the herbs in the ancient leather bag. 'Could it be,' she said, 'that if the Grimoire has changed between threads that the herbs may have too?'

'It's possible but how would that manifest?'

'Let's look through the packages carefully, although they don't have labels that are readable...' Vanessa trailed off. 'Okay, where do we start?'

'Well, Cal has put them into categories and alphabetically too, which should narrow the field for the specific herbs we might need for the Mabon rite.'

Flora had many times combed through the ancient bag of herbs given her by Airmhid, her patron Goddess of herbs, healing and Magick, but there were still so many unidentifiable. Without knowing what they were she was unusually indecisive about using any at all, fearing they may be toxic.

'What if what we gave Sam to take, the mistletoe and the mugwort combined, made her vanish again to this thread?'

'Flo, you can't be serious, Sam not grabbing the bracelet that was more likely the cause. You have to be positive Flo, we can't give up the search for her or Sybille and then there's Morgan to think of. Where did he vanish to?'

'I know Nessa; I think its hormones making me so nervy. It's as if I've become a different person entirely; I hardly know myself.'

'We know you though Flo,' said Cal walking in from the garden. 'What you're experiencing is normal.'

'I do know that love, after all the women I've seen through the process. It's just so different from this perspective, but this isn't getting anything done to find Sam is it?'

'Okay, so what have you decided?'

'We're about to take a look through Airmhid's herbs to see if anything has changed because the Grimoire has these funny markings, bird scratching's, all over the pages; look.'

'Well, they look as if they form a pattern of sorts,' said Cal reaching for a magnifying glass. 'It's like music somehow but nothing I've ever seen before.' He scrunched up his face in concentration.

At that moment, Beth wandered in. 'What's going on? I could hear weird music coming from in here.'

'I can't hear anything more than a sort of buzzing but come look at this Bethy,' said Vanessa, 'it's really odd what's happening to the Grimoire. I went to look at Nina's copy, as you know, which I guess is the original. When I woke up on the floor the Grimoire had come back with me. I thought it might alter it the way the original changed and wanted to look at it at the cottage in case and it seems it *has* changed, just not the same way. We were about to look at the herbs to see if anything had changed there too.'

'Alright, where do we start?'

Cal replied, 'I've categorised them so if we start with the bundles for protection, curse breaking…'

'*Curse breaking*!' Vanessa and Flo echoed in unison, Beth looked stunned.

'Well, that's what we're up against I would imagine, or similar. Protection alone isn't enough to stop Aelish doing her dark Magicks so we have to have a counter action to halt her spell in its tracks.'

'When did you get so cluey about Magick, Cal?' Beth grinned, 'You're a sly one aren't you?'

'It must have rubbed off being around all you weirdoes,' he grinned.

'It's just the word *curse* that makes me nervous. Mum's ah …affliction, the blight and the sting from the Dark Maker could be a curse.' Vanessa shivered at the thought. 'What's Aelish's reason though, other than fancying Bran? Why would that turn someone …well, *bad*?'

'Most importantly why would that degree of negativity be there in the first place? I mean what caused it?' Bethan paused, 'Okay, what is the one thing that makes a curse work and what is the one thing that stops it; Vanessa?'

'Erm …belief that curses work and I'd have to say living here; safety in numbers; you know!'

'Flo?'

'Yes, agreed, belief that curses work, but also self-confidence to know we're strong enough to beat it when we do get jittery and feeling safe? Hmm, the herbs, the knowledge held in the Grimoire but I'd feel even better if we could find Sybille's Book of Shadows.'

'Cal?'

'I think this sort of curse has so much potency, more than we can imagine but I believe in us. That makes me feel protected.'

'So what object do you possess that would add to the sense of power and strength?' Beth asked them in turn.

'All the tools Maeve has made and the ones we've made for ourselves and the belief in our own strengths,' said Vanessa.

'Exactly!' Beth exclaimed. 'Tools of power, sacred objects of power and things like knowledge and trust; everything Sybille ever taught us.'

'Now has anyone seen Maeve or Alma? We need to call the others. Somehow, we have to get the Mabon rite together at the same time as Ostara and already be heading for the final rituals at Samhain here and Beltane in Glastonbury. Hercurin said we must have a completion by then.'

'Do you think we should split into two groups?' asked Cal. 'I guess there's more power in one group working though.'

To everyone's surprise, Beth reached over to grab Cal's ears, pulling him close to kiss him full on the lips. 'You, my friend are a genius. Two groups, of course, and that means we work from both sides of the Planet. Two Equinox, autumn, spring, then Samhain and Beltane, the directions will be interesting,' she said excitedly, 'two cross quarter and two quarter festivals but somehow we should be able to achieve a balance.'

'Who should be where, do you think?' Cal responded.

'Well, the obvious would be Lily, Max, Robyn and then there's Maeve and Jamie in the UK. Here we have Claire plus Pwyll, if he sticks around long enough and us four, which leaves my parents who we wouldn't want to separate.'

'That makes an odd number though,' said Vanessa thoughtfully, 'but if we left your parents here and I went to the UK it would even the numbers. My energies increase as soon as I'm anywhere near the Tor and the cottage which seems to be somewhere close to Robyn's farm.'

'Is there someone Robyn knows and trusts, Beth?' asked Flora.

'We could ask Robyn about Rose Dane. She's back in the UK and living in Somerset too.'

'Isn't she a close friend to Sybille and part of the Grove? I remember Mum talking about her; they were friends too,' Vanessa replied.

Beth paused before answering; 'Yes, she and Sybille were great friends and Claire and Susan know her well; they all studied the craft together. That could work if Rose is willing, although it seems a bit late to be bringing new energy into the mix.'

'We could use some new energy Beth,' said Cal. 'We're all depleted with Morgan and Sam gone and Rose is experienced, I would think. Let's face it we need all the help we can get and there's no one else we know well enough to trust. All the other Grove members hived off with Annie after Sybille vanished; sorry Vanessa,' he added gently, seeing her face fall, 'and we all saw what happened there. At least Rose, from what I've heard, was strong enough to stand up to her.'

'Okay, does she know about shapers though? We don't want anyone collapsing in fear at the sight if anyone had to make a sudden change.'

'If she knows Mum, Beth' said Flora, 'I'm sure she'd know.'

'Let's get this settled with Robyn and the others, but it would much simpler as long as we don't all have to experience both hemispheres to make it work,' Beth sighed. 'We need a meet as soon as possible so let's contact Robyn through the portal to organise it for tomorrow after work.'

'This is it,' said Vanessa. 'I can feel it, although it will be very strange to be there instead of here, I'm so drawn to the UK and to Nina's cottage. I think it must be there somewhere on another thread but perhaps it still exists?'

'We forget something,' said Flora. 'Aithlin and Aerandir and all the Elven clan.'

'We won't get to organise them Nessa,' Cal laughed. 'They're a law unto themselves but I would say Aerandir is likely to go where you go and where Nina is closer energetically; Aithlin would be here with Beth.'

'…and this would mean seven per circle. Perfect for protection and a banishing,' finished Flora.

'Or a Curse removal.' Cal grinned.

'Ha! Tell that to the birds.' Flora quipped, 'Now, where were we? Ah yes, the scratchy marks on the pages. What did you hear Beth?'

'I can still hear it; it has a strange rhythm to it that's nothing I've ever known. If you keep moving the pages or packets about, it increases.'

'Hey, do you think it would record if we were to use that little device Morgan has?' Cal queried.

'We could try it tomorrow at work, or did Morgan keep it at Wells? Beth, do you know?' said Vanessa.

'I can't remember, I'll check when I get back but for now let's see if we can make sense of the markings.'

Flora pulled the bag toward her, carefully opening it again, taking out the packets in the neat bundles Cal had so meticulously worked on. The first bore the label Protection in his neat handwriting. Then there was Banishing, Cleansing, Healing, Drawing and many others: Prosperity, Glamour, Pain, Abundance, Tranquillity, Meditation, Circle Casting, Clearing; an endless list of precious herbs and blends, some of which they'd documented and used at previous rites.

Many were easily identifiable: elderflower and berries; hawthorn flower and berries; rosehips and petals from a wild rose so ancient yet the perfume lingered and the petals were velvety soft as if they were slowly reconstituting themselves. There was elecampane, poppy seed, mistletoe berries, vervain, wild violet, lily of the valley root, orrisroot and belladonna, wolfs bane, sage and so the list went on.

'Well,' said Cal, 'at least we made a start cataloguing, but there are still so many that I have no idea about.'

With each packet they removed, the ringing tones of the musical language became louder and as they looked they saw the same scratched markings on the labels.

'Shit, where do we begin?' Flora almost rang her hands in frustration.

'It's getting late, sis. Come on, let's get to bed and make a fresh start in the morning.'

'Agreed,' Beth yawned loudly, stretching. 'I'm going to head home.' She hugged each of them in turn. 'Night guys.'

'Night Beth, see you at work tomorrow. I'll bring the bag with me and Nessa's going to take another look for the Book of Shadows.'

Cal stood a moment as Beth's car headlights cut a swathe through the mist. Other creatures stirred, following her; to protect, Cal wondered or was it simply, for the love of the beautiful Fae creature she was.

Chapter 19
Inroads to Understanding

They are small ...their wings are frail
...once subtle green ...they're now so pale
They are so tired and need to sleep
...she'll bury down into the deep
How will they live in all the smoke and dust?
...the driving rains ...earth's rumbling crust
Where will they go ...fragile as snow?
As you believe, so are they real
You may not see them, but you can feel
...if you say no, they'll simply go
...simply disappear into the flow

That night Vanessa and Flora woke at the same moment. Vanessa had once again been travelling in fox shape through a frozen landscape, while Flora found herself sitting at the table with the bag of herbs, the Grimoire and strangely, Sybille's original Book of Shadows.

Drawn downstairs, Flora left Cal sleeping, pausing briefly to look at his sleeping form. Since his experience with his aspect, Ivor, Cal had changed. He had always been a tall and well-built man but now his body was that of a young, strong archer, muscles clearly etched and defined. All she really wanted was to crawl back into bed and curl up close to him but the urgent need to go downstairs and work was too strong a pull to resist.

Vanessa reached the bag and Grimoire at the same moment as Flora and they sat together, taking out each bundle again. Wordlessly they saw the inscriptions, more sharply etched than the night before; haunting chirrups filled their senses, stirring their hearts and minds. They exchanged bemused glances as tiny birds gathered, wings rustling with a susurrus, eerie sound, not unlike the crunching noise of the dried herbs hanging over the counter in the kitchen or in Flora's drying room.

Several Fae, changing from bird form to their curious twiggy shapes, diaphanous wings folding behind them, made the same whispering noise. They approached each package with reverence, carefully studying the inscriptions. They opened several bundles in order to study each individual herb. Slowly they worked their way through every single pack, separating some out to create new groups not typically used together.

Hours past and dawn approached on silent wings of song. They were rudely interrupted by a clatter on the roof as the morning group of noisy Raven who put in an appearance weren't their usual cheeky selves. They sat watching the small Fae with stern gazes and the Fae began a song of nervous clicks and rustles until, one by one, they faded from sight.

The Raven left also, all but one, larger and fiercer than any they'd come across. There

was no warmth or kindness in the piercing blue eyes, only disapproval. It was cold enough to shrivel their courage; icier than The Morrigan's dark eyed stare.

'What did we *do*?' Vanessa called out when she found her tongue again. 'We're just trying to find Sam and Morgan.'

'Your task is only to find Sybille,' the cold reply made Vanessa shrink back in surprise.

'But without them we have less chance of finding her and we want all our friends home safe.'

'Do not question the Morrigan, child. Find one and you find all.' With that, the huge shaper flew away with a raucous call to its siblings.

Flora let out a loud puff of air, 'That's told us then! I don't get it Nessa, we need all of them home safely and if we're given the task of finding Sybille then surely, after all we've been through, it's up to us how we go about it and where we find the help we need. Goddess only knows that's been short on the ground,' she growled.

'I agree Flo, but maybe the help we just got from the little shapers is exactly what caused this reaction. Perhaps they were acting off their own bat, not because they were told to.'

'Hmm, you could have a point there. There always seems to be ulterior motives to everything and personally, I'm over all the underhanded, convoluted events of the last years. I want to get this done and done now! I don't *care* anymore what the 'otherworldly' creatures think either. Now, let's get some breakfast and head into work. We can take the herbs with us because I have some time to look at why they separated out the ones they did. They make a very curious blend and possibly volatile so I'm hoping no one has to actually ingest them.'

Cal walked in at that moment, thrusting his hands through tawny hair grown long and curling. He pulled a warm fleece on, yawning widely.

'Aaah, did I hear something about breakfast?' he ruffled Flora's hair, hugging her in his unselfconscious way.

'Yes you did and good morning love,' smiled Flo. 'Nessa and I are heading into work. We had some strange occurrences this morning so even more reason to get together with the others tonight.'

While Flora cooked breakfast and Nessa laid the table they told Cal of the happenings earlier. He made no response, just nodded occasionally, chewing thoughtfully.

Slowly, one by one the little Fae returned. They remained hunched in their bird forms on the back of chairs and any other handy perch.

Chapter 20
Herbal Rites and Rights

One of the Tuatha De Danaan, Airmhid, is the sacred healer and herbalist of the Fae folk. She is the daughter of Dian Cecht, the divine physician of the Tuatha De Danaan.

They are the keepers of a Magickal healing well (surely that must be the Lady's Well in Glastonbury, Cal made note) where wounded warriors are brought after a battle. When washed in the well they emerged healed in mind, body, emotions and spirit.

Airmhid and her brother Miach healed the chief of the Tuatha De, Nuada of the Silverhand and so proved their miraculous abilities, causing their father, Dian Cecht, to lose his superiority as the divine physician. He then challenged Miach to a competition, which resulted in Miach's death.

Three hundred and sixty five healing plants grew from Miach's grave and so Airmhid picked and dried them, pinning them to her cloak so they would always be nearby to heal all. Dian Cecht snatched the cloak from Airmhid and some of the herbs were scattered. It is believed had this not occurred we would have the knowledge of every herb to heal all illness and disease. Now those missing plants are part of the search for remedies that are arcane, secret knowledge, which only Airmhid knows.

Patron Lady of herbalists and healers, she is petitioned as a mediator for people who are struck by illnesses that have no known cures. Healers call on her in healing Magicks, when learning herbalism and about family loyalties. Together with her broth-

Cal put down his pen to rub at tired eyes. After Flo and Nessa had left for work he sat to revise all the notes he'd made on the Goddess Airmhid and was busy cross-referencing her association with the Goddesses Aynia and Arianrhod. His thought processes were to find any possible links through either or all of them with Sybille and The Cybil. He sensed they were missing something in the whole picture and that it was exactly that missing something, which would unlock why Sybille was a target in the first place or whether she was merely a pawn in the game. He wanted an opportunity to ask Robyn or Tara, if she was feeling more herself, if there were ever moments in the journey to renew when the Littleshape was more vulnerable. 'Who,' he thought, continuing the thread he'd begun, 'would most likely take advantage of that moment?' It was no easier keeping the secret to himself knowing where Sybille may be but not what had happened in the first place.

Sighing he continued perusing his neatly penned notes...

When he read these notes, written two years ago, he realised the connection little Alma may well have with the Lady Aynia. Alma was, or had been, such a collector of anything that sparkled and in his mind, he called her the

Magpie Faery. Had she perhaps moved one too many rocks, shells or seaweed-entangled treasures from the rocky coastline that was Aynia's precinct? Come to that, where had Alma actually come from? Yes, she'd been a child snatched by Aelish and changed from promising seer-child to a wild water sprite, a Merrow. Which had come first? There must have been the changer essence present in the child and the child present in the changer.

He stretched, yawning; several hours had passed and the sun had come out. It was a crisp, bright autumn day again, the kind he loved the most and the garden called, at least for a while.

Changing into heavy boots, he grabbed a pair of thick gloves and secateurs; he thought he would begin tidying the bramble hedges. Ripe berries nestled under the prickly canopy of green so he collected a soft wire basket to pick the fruit as he went. Tomorrow he would surprise Flo with some bottles of syrup and perhaps there was enough for some blackberry wine. Then there were the grapes hanging in shiny, moisture-coated colours. Not long before harvest.

Head down, busy with his tasks, he sensed rather than saw a presence in his peripheral vision. He'd not seen her up close before but both Sam, Flo and Nessa had interacted with her; Nessa just yesterday when she'd journeyed to Nina's cottage. Surrounded by many tiny beings, shapers, just like the ones he'd seen that morning, she kept her distance, studying him seriously.

Cal smiled and nodded respectfully but she made no move to respond, merely staring at and through him, fiercely.

In his head he heard the words, first in a strange language common to all the little-kin and then in his own tongue. 'You have been busy with your thoughts and they do not lead you astray but then again the Greenlord has given his blessing and so you remain stoically silent when it could all be over and your friends safe at home.'

Cal felt distinctly disgruntled, tired of being judged. 'If the Greenlord had not told me I must not disclose where Sybille is hidden I would have shared long ago and short circuited all the coming and going, perhaps even spared Sam all the pain she's had to know.'

'Ah yes, noble of you Cal but have you thought that the experience Sam is having she would have to experience in a different form in order for her to remember all she is?'

'True, I see that and tussle with it constantly but if there is one being who could hold my tongue still, it's Hercurin.'

'In that you are indeed wise, young Ivor,' and she vanished, a trail of birds and sprites followed.

'What was that about?' he thought aloud. Turning, he saw he had yet another visitor. This time it was Silver, her hair streaming, her garments rent and her gaping belly appeared to be full of swirling dark worlds full of blight and a blackened, ichorous substance. She looked paler

than ice and wept as she wandered, apparently lost to all
but her own pain now.

He sighed deeply as he felt her raw pain and help-
lessness. 'All right, enough! Time for some action.'

Putting away his tools, he went back inside gathering
the Grimoire, his notes and the bag of herbs, carefully
keeping aside those the Fae had separated out and headed
into town to bring the group together. No time for mundane work now. Between them, they could afford to put a
crew of staff on to look after 'earthly rites'. There was no
more time to lose and no more ball-breaking over what
they didn't know; merely working with what they did
would just have to be enough. They each had skills that
went beyond the ordinary so no more playing coy either
and no time for fear.

As he walked with his load to the car, he paused.
'Okay, bring it on!' as he punched his fist to the sky.

Hercurin chuckled to himself from the forest edge.
'Ah boy, about time indeed.' He stroked the little Nature
Sprite gently and she blossomed under his touch, then
fleet of foot, he ran through the autumn sunlight calling
his kin to the hunt, so close he could smell it now.

Chapter 21
An Unbreakable Vow

When promises made, we cannot keep
...there comes a reckoning to rob our sleep
When we lie for gain, a broken vow runs deep
...in the end all that remains is to weep

Aelish stood, hands on her hips, a sneer of derision etching lines on her once beautiful features as she looked down at the man cowering at her feet. How easy it was to bend the weak-willed human simply by wearing Annie's face like a mask over her own.

Harry wept; the strong, pompous demeanour of his 'surgeon self' buried and forgotten in his guilt and fear as he realised the success promised him and achieved, had been in return for Annie's vows made to Aelish. He tried to gather his thoughts, to bargain that Annie had made the promises of her own choosing and not because of his involvement with her, but he knew it would be pointless. The deal was sealed the moment Annie had dedicated herself willingly to a creature she believed to be a Goddess. Aelish had seized the moment to throw her glamour over her and Annie, not coerced, was egotistical enough to be flattered by being a 'chosen one.'

Now he knelt a broken man and if he wished to keep the façade of his career, he would have to continue being the plaything of the sneering creature he saw Aelish to be.

'Where is it?' she screeched at him. 'Sybille's book; do you have it?' Her sounding of Sybille's name was as sibilant as a snake's hiss.

Harry fell forward at the venom in her words, flattening himself to the ground further, wishing it would swallow him. In his weakness, he feared she would see though his lie. He saw images of another man sprawled on the floor in agony but couldn't put a name to the face, quite similar to his own, although dark and swarthy. He swallowed his fear; it tasted of bitter vetch. 'No, Lady,' he whispered hoarsely, almost retching, 'it's still hidden somewhere. I hear it whisper to me, but I swear I can't find it and Vanessa caught me snooping around Annie's things and threw me out.'

'So a mere girl can throw a man out of his lover's house without him putting up a fight. What sort of weak being are you?' She spat contemptuously. Apparently his lie had gone undetected and he closed his eyes lest she see his small triumph.

'Get up and get out of my sight,' she spat. Vanishing, she left him on his knees somewhere in the veil. Annie's shade circled him once, but he was blind to her efforts to help him. She whispered to him and hoped he would hear.

'Go to Italy, Harry. She cannot cross water except through the veil and first she must find you. La Stregga will help you be invisible to her; she too needs to make amends for lives lost to this creature's ill will.'

Harry woke to find himself in his own bed. He retched, rolling out of bed he fled to the bathroom. Coughing and rinsing his mouth, he spat the bitter tasting bile into the sink. Blue-black lines snaked over his neck and chest briefly, but he didn't see them, focused as he was on the blood staining his spittle in the sink. Too stunned to react, he walked blindly to the front door when he heard the rattle of mail through the letterbox. A letter with a foreign postmark drew his immediate attention. He ripped the envelope open; Italy; a job offer in Italy, teaching at the university in Florence, an answer to a prayer

'Thank you, Annie,' he whispered as a gentle touch stroked his cheek.

Harry Jenkins felt he was going home. Another thread waited where a man, wrought with grief, wept over his comatose daughter and a black clad 'Dottore' said, 'I agree, we cannot bleed her, Signorina Nina is already too weak.'

His last attempt to make amends was to write a note to Vanessa, telling his story without glossing over the truths as he saw them. He didn't leave a forwarding address but wrote that he would let her know when he was settled, making no mention of Italy. He feared Aelish would track him down, or worse, turn her attention to the daughter he hardly knew. Praying Aelish would not pick up the sounds on the aether, he put the Book of Shadows in a metal box. Alongside, wrapped in silk, he placed the wand he'd snatched from Vanessa; he'd not given it to Aelish despite his fear of her. He hoped they would remain hidden from the Dark Fae and her minions.

Chapter 22
Action Plans

Flying the winds, no time to think clearly
Mabon approaches, autumn begins yearly
Golden leaves shine before the world becomes bleary
Through vision gone white, a scream rips the night
…the need fire burning bright dispels the dreary

Bethan sat at her loom, weaving a vibrant blend of colour; an autumn wrap for a client. Forgoing the trip to Springsmeet, she preferred to spend the day finishing what she'd started in the way of orders and was content to be alone before the meet tonight at Robyn's farm.

Singing quietly to herself, the yarns became a blur in front of her eyes. She could hear the clack of the loom as she moved the shuttle back and forth, back and forth, as always, hypnotic. Her mind shifted to golden days when she'd travelled to work and learnt from her mentor Sybille; how long ago it seemed.

Suddenly, vision gone, she was blind, cringing in a hollow of an ancient tree and yet it felt as if it were only her body, an empty shell, a husk of her former self. Panic stricken, she realised there was no feeling in her extremities at all. A soothing voice called to her and she slept on, oblivious to the women who searched for her desperately but who were almost ready to give up the fight.

Gasping, conscious of whom she'd seen for just a moment, Beth knew Sybille's body was in peril and without a body there was nowhere to go. Recovering herself she left her loom and rushed to her car. Beth raced into town to hasten the process of the meet. Like Cal, she knew there was no more time to waste; if time there was, it had all run out.

Reaching the store, Beth rushed in. Vanessa was at the desk training a young girl who had applied for work while she was finishing school. Her available time, with exams over, were more hours than they had to give, but suddenly it all made sense, falling into place as the realisation struck; there was no more time.

Vanessa's friends had also made themselves available and she remembered the day she'd brought them in for a reading. Her friend had been turning eighteen and it had been a gift from the group to her. She also remembered how embarrassed she was when she discovered that her mother didn't own the business but had led her to believe she did.

Cal arrived at the same time as Beth, both with the same urgency that staff be trained and the crew spend what time was left to them focusing only on bringing their friends home.

Bursting into the apothecary, where Flora stood mixing a tincture for a client, Beth only had to look at her for Flora to say, 'Okay, I just need to finish this and I'm there. I've already cleared my schedule for the next few weeks. Something told me we must spend all the time we have left to see this finished. It must be done!'

Cal went straight to Vanessa at the reception desk. 'I know,' she said. 'Trish is ready to run the front desk and Andrea, mum's old friend, is ready for anything. She's smart enough to know that mum's death was not in any way normal and will do all she can to put things straight. She has our back; between the two of them they will cope, so we can get on with things.'

After finding Flora, Beth went upstairs to see if Maeve was in her studio. She found her at her bench, working on an exquisite piece of silver, forged in the shape of a dragonfly, one of her personal Sigels. A look from Beth had her scrambling to get a few things together. She included the last pieces of the crystal shards that had fallen into her possession so easily, causing her much grief in the making of a wand and snood for Beth. No matter that now, it was time to leave all else behind and get the job done.

She contacted Jamie on the aether. They were as close to telepathic communication as anyone Beth had ever come across, as were Lily and Max, except perhaps when Hercurin called her; she grinned blissfully to herself.

'What was that?' Maeve chuckled. 'I felt I had to leave the room to give you a private moment.'

'Oh, well your ability to communicate with Jamie got me thinking of; you know,' her blush had Maeve crowing with laughter. 'Come on then, you ready?'

'Absolutely. Jamie will be waiting at Robyn's by the time we collect everyone.'

Susan and Alex would meet them there when they could; both had taken time off work when they heard the urgency in Beth's voice. They could now easily travel through the painting's portal to Greenman Ways and since she'd painted it, Susan's work was becoming more and more complex. People were seeking out her art, unaware of the hidden gateways the Onceborn could not see or experience.

Lily and Max were keen to get on with it all too. Lily missed Morgan desperately; they'd not been far apart for much of their lives. Pwyll had been hanging around a lot lately, but she just couldn't bring herself to forgive him, particularly now they knew their mother's identity. She was, on the one hand, disgusted and, on the other, intrigued. It was a disconcerting feeling, which left her disturbed to think where her own lethal temperament, her darker side, had come from.

Chapter 23
Confusion

A web of lies, a pool of tears
...drowning in mortal fears
What lies were told, what deals were made
Who walks the path from Chalice bright
...to dark-edged blade?

During the journey to Robyn's, each immersed in her or his own thoughts, everyone felt they were readying for battle, but threads were starting to unravel. No light-hearted singing this time as they walked

Vanessa thought about the past weeks and her mother's death. She was aware that her mother, gullible and egotistical as she had been, fell victim to a different intention altogether. Harry was a strange bedfellow; she shuddered at the thought of how she had come into being, her mother would be aware her best friend's husband was taboo.

What and who had been the reasons for her desperate need for recognition? Vanessa could only imagine it had come from her childhood; having never met her Italian grandparents, she could only assume. More was at stake now; too many lives were affected by one woman's ego. Where would it all end?

Her earlier search for the Book of Shadows finally rewarded, she held the heavy box close to her chest in a sturdy leather bag. She'd previously caught glimpses of it, as if it were there but hidden and only when she looked out the corner of her eye could she see it. Tonight she'd reveal it to the others, her need to keep it hidden until reaching Robyn's paramount; she couldn't let it be seen or heard as they passed through the veil. Her father's note had explained more about the Dark Fae, Aelish and his and her mother's role in all the tangled Skeins.

Her quiet thoughts continued…

'I can't believe that she's gone …mum's gone. Thank the Goddess for my sister; I wouldn't have known how to cope. She helped me hold myself together but was also there when everything fell apart. Goddess bless Claire and Cal too.

Ah, Claire, mother of my heart, she is so good to accept me as Flo's half-sister, knowing her husband had an affair and with one of her best friends too. What possessed either of them, mum or Harry, is beyond me; I wouldn't exactly see Harry as a 'catch', despite his fame as a surgeon. I've never seen mum as a particularly passionate person; I wonder who the instigator was?'

For the first time ever she called him Dad in her thoughts. She'd read the letter she'd found when she dashed back for another look, together with a heavy metal box. Both were sitting on the Altar with her mum's tools. He'd bought a new bag and had placed all of them inside. Each tool was mute. No sound of her mother's song remained, but she felt lifted when she read the note. Opening the lid of the box, she saw the Book of Shadows nestling inside and a smaller, silk-wrapped object, which hummed with subtle power. She knew without looking it was the wand she'd found among her mum's things. So Harry had at least finally done the right thing. When she returned she'd reconsecrate her mother's tools for her own; rededicate them to the Goddess of Fox energy. She would ask Jamie who that was. Flidais perhaps?

Now, clutching both box and note to her, she let her thoughts drift on; it seemed as if they walked for hours.

Carrying the shards in her backpack, Maeve could hear the sounds becoming stronger as they moved through the Skeins. She could hear the notes of her friend's thoughts somewhat discordantly as each battled their own inner demons. She didn't have to ask where Vanessa's thoughts had strayed…

'Poor girl,' she thought compassionately. 'What it would be like, I wonder, to have a normal childhood, normal parents. At least mum's alive, although barely, considering how she lives. When this is all over, I'll surprise her with a visit and see if I can convince her to come to live in Springsmeet. I can spend some of the money from the sale of the studio to pay for her rehab.'

Suddenly the strange sounds she'd heard grew stronger when Flo moved closer to her. 'What are you carrying Flo? The crystals are going crazy every time you move closer to me.'

'Airmhid's bag with the herbs and the Grimoire,' she replied. 'Other than that, just some clothes, tools and my robe. I wonder if the scribble on the herb labels and all over the Grimoire are triggering a response in the shards. We'll have to check it out tomorrow.'

While she waited for her friends to arrive at the store, Lily had a moment to herself. She was not aware of anything that happened after the standoff between Claire and her Da. She wished, it had been her who had the courage to confront him but she, torn between what she perceived and what in effect she knew, was gutted. Only Max had even thought to take the time to care what she felt. Confusion and guilt consumed her when she considered everything at stake, but she was so tired of thinking of everyone else's pain when she was drowning in her own.

She had time for a walk; the shop was closed for the day. Max was busy working on his manuscript; sorely neglected of late. Her feet took her over the hills and there by the Chalice well, Aelish found her moment, whispering words Lily to encourage rage and disgust toward her father rather than she see who her mother truly was. Aelish would go to great lengths to win a daughter to her who was malleable and scared, particularly as she'd lost Nina, her one hope for attaining all she'd dreamed.

Lily was no fool, aware of who stood in the shadows as the last piece of the jigsaw fell into place for her, when Claire and Pwyll had called her, *'her.'* She had known without a doubt that the shade who haunted everyone was her mother. Alicia, suddenly she remembered her name and she was convinced if Nessa spoke with Nina, her mother would be of the same name or similar. Another thread, another space in time but the same corrupted spirit.

A sudden noise behind her had Lily turning rapidly; Alma appeared from the well itself. Beth had sent her to the Seer's Isle, but it was hidden away in thick Mysts that even she couldn't penetrate and so she'd gone to Robyn's to wait for the group to arrive. Robyn was busy with something so she took herself off to the hideaway beneath the well, thinking perhaps Sam-Rowan, might be there again.

'It's dangerous here Jay-Lily,' Alma took her hand. 'The others are on their way. I'll walk back with you.' She tugged Lily along with more strength than would be expected of such a slender child. 'We can go straight to Robyn's from here if you want?'

'I have to pick Max up on the way and the others are arriving through the portal, so come back with me and we can walk with them to Robyn's.'

Glancing over her shoulder nervously and baring her neat, rather pointed teeth every now and then, Alma concurred. She slipped her hand in Lily's to walk back to Greenman Ways to wait for the crew.

Cal too was deep in his own thoughts as he walked through the veil…

*'I know my parents were the same for both aspects, Ivor
and me now, but where and why had everything gone wrong
for them? In this thread, I couldn't have wished for better
parents. I still can't understand why on both threads they had
such terrible deaths. When I spoke of curse breaking with
Nessa and Flo before, I wondered about the random truth of
my own words. I will never forget the face of the Dark Fae;
it's easy to see who the source of all our trials is. Who was the
trigger though, that was the question? Now there's no more
time to waste, everything will come to a head sooner rather
than later. I can smell her over everything.'*

Maeve was surprised to find Alma waiting at the
store, believing her safely ensconced with The Cybil by
now. She knew her child was loathe to leave them, but it
was dangerous for her to be anywhere near Aelish. 'What
happened love?' she asked Alma as calmly as she could,
though her nerves were jumping.

'It's gone Mam, disappeared where even I couldn't
go. The Cybil is hiding a secret.'

'What makes you say that?'

'Well Beth and I… we went to the Isle and it had
vanished in the Mysts, we saw the First Born though. I'm
sure it was Sam and Morgan, and Tara was there too but
she was her well self.' Alma rambled, words tumbling out.

'What do you mean, Sam and Morgan were there
and Tara's at Robyn's, you saw her there yesterday.'

'We all live on many threads at the same time Mam;
you know that,' Alma finished, triumphantly grinning.

'Okay, you win,' Maeve said, attempting to get her head around it all. Despite her experiences, it still made her dizzy to think of all the aspects of herself moving around in the aethers hidden from each other.

'Wait a minute!' she exclaimed; the thought brought her to a standstill, the others walking behind almost fell over her. 'When I was taken by Tara to Scathach's hearth, I remember thinking that if I'm on that thread, did I have parents there or was I just literally transported to where I had no aspect. After all, we can't meet our own aspects face to face on the same thread easily. Even Bran and Morgan communicated through their minds when they spoke with The Cybil, which means I'm an anomaly. It means I can go anywhere, other than the thread where I was a young girl who fell in love with a foxy-lad.' She paused, realising everyone had stopped to listen to her ramblings; she grinned sheepishly.

'Genius,' said Cal. 'You're not a shifter as far as we know. Alma is your child from that thread and we all know how tragic that tale is but somehow, you've just stumbled on a link we hadn't thought of. Genius!' he repeated, hugging her fiercely.

'Okay, I'm not sure where my thoughts are going with this or where it will take us but maybe we should go to Scathach's hearth and see if we can get to the Isle from that thread. Perhaps, with Bran now firmly connected within Morgan, we can scry and find him which will find Morgan.'

'Genius,' Jamie appeared from nowhere; tousled Maeve's hair and grinning broadly, hoisted Alma to his shoulders.

'I knew we were close to something,' Cal said to Jamie. 'Now I sense we are off on a tangent which will take us closer to where we're trying to go but can't yet see.'

'Yeah, what you said Cal.' Jamie clapped him on the shoulder and they walked the rest of the way through the ways Between.

Chapter 24
Maeve Walks Alone

As the seasons change and the year moves on
...listen closely, in the forest there's a wistful song.
Although it's fading now as the windswept skies
...blows a covering of leaves for where she lies
...to sleep away the chilly hours
...in woodland glade and dappled bowers.
Where small creatures flock to see her there
...tying feathers and flowers in her fading hair
...to watch her sleep and wait for spring
...when once again they'll hear her sing

Maeve took the route Between through the portal but instead of going through to the shop in Glastonbury she paused a moment. She'd never done this before, not alone and she wasn't sure what she was supposed to be looking out for anyway. A sign perhaps ...something simple she thought or would she try to call one of the Hearth to guide her there, although then it would have to be a seer.

She waited, not wanting to just step through unaware of what faced her. A strange whooshing sound approached and she all but dived back through the portal.

The way shower who appeared was a welcome sight. Bran walked with light-footed confidence, a grin from ear to ear on his face. 'You called, M'lady?' he bowed mockingly.

'What brings you here, Bran?' she said hugging him as an old friend would.

'You did Maeve. Morgan let me know you were on the way through.'

'But how did he know? We haven't seen him since Sam disappeared again.'

'He and I are constantly in communication. What he hears, I hear and the reverse is true.'

'That doesn't answer my question Bran.'

'Ah, perhaps it's the birds then,' Bran grinned again, lighter than she'd known him before. 'It must be the connection to Morgan,' she thought.

'Now walk with me Maeve and we'll be in Scathach's Hearth before night fall. In the morning we'll head for the Isle; Leah will be waiting.'

On reaching the Hearth, the other women she'd trained with greeted Maeve with friendly nods and waves and the children she'd instructed rushed at her with unconcealed joy. They asked her if she were back for good and would she teach them something new. A quiet, gifted boy by the name of Ivor looked on and smiled. Bran head for the Hearth, unpacking his harp as he walked to a spot set up for him.

Out the corner of her eye, Maeve spotted Alma sneaking through the gathering with a full plate of food.

Maeve yelled, 'Hey weren't you supposed to stay at home to polish the sparkly things?'

Alma grinned, 'I'm not really here Mam. You're imagining me,' then vanished with a chime of laughter.

'Kids,' Maeve muttered; the girl leading her to Scathach looked bemused. 'Oh, you know, their enthusiasm is all.' She covered her tracks quickly. Of course, no one else had seen Alma; if they did, they would think her a shade, for on this thread the little girl was lost to them.

On reaching the Hearth fire, Scathach hugged Maeve like a long, lost daughter, sharing her own choice cuts of meat and crusty bread. Breaking bread always took precedence over business, not that Maeve had any to conduct other than some gifts of simple tools, whetstones for sharpening blades and such.

As she politely shared the meal, leaving the last for her mentor, saying she was full, Maeve noticed a strange woman eyeing her from across the fire pit. Unsure of who she was, Maeve didn't want to be caught staring rudely but felt disconcerted by the woman's direct gaze. Without making a show, Maeve leaned surreptitiously closer to her companion on the left and asked if she knew who the woman was.

'Why that's Flidais, some say a Goddess indeed and not to be crossed. She comes on occasion to break bread with the Lady Scathach. They are blood sisters and hunt together often. She loves to watch the young men fight and hunt and some say...,' the girl giggled behind her hand, but too late to avoid Scathach's glance, eyebrow raised, before continuing in a muted voice. 'They say she does more than watch them at sport too.'

'Well, thank you,' Maeve replied politely, pretending to stretch and yawn. Turning to Scathach, she said, 'Forgive me my Lady, may I take my leave to sleep I will be gone early in the morning to the Seer's Isle.'

Scathach nodded her assent and went back to her food and conversation. As Maeve walked through the Tuath she knew she was followed and by whom. Not usually nervous when walking through the familiar place, she swallowed her fears and called out. 'I hear and smell you Lady, would you show yourself, rather than skulk in the shadows.

'Flidais does not skulk child; mind your manners. I am to assist you it would seem. A new changer has made her first shift and she is close to the one known as Jamie. You, of course, know him well, being hand fasted and all. I hear your child is safe and well but don't think I didn't see her slipping through the Tuath like a shade.' Flidais smiled, but there was a definite edge to the smile, revealing pearly white teeth that appeared sharp and fang like for a moment, reminding her of Alma. 'She and I have a few issues to sort out but that's for another time.'

'Lady, my apologies if the child has offended you but she is that, a child.'

'You think Alma is a child? Then she has you fooled.'

'I know she is Lady as I gave her birth on a thread in the Skeins; her Da, is Jamie the Foxy-lad,' she met Flidais' glare without blinking, 'and also on other threads such as here when she was lost to us all, taken by the full moon King tides. She has haunted me in her Merrow aspect on another thread and now she is …was there, staying with friends. She has grown and changed Lady; you wouldn't know her. Soon she will be a young woman.'

'Sadly,' Flidais took Maeve's hand unexpectedly, 'she has never seen adulthood.'

Maeve froze, not wanting to hear what this abrasive Goddess had to say but forced, through respect, to do so. She made no reply though.

'I do not wish to hurt you Maeve that is not what I want to speak with you about. Jamie is one of my Firstborn, as is the one who wakes now, an aspect to Ni-na, also of my clan and kin.'

Maeve, sucking in her breath in surprise, replied, 'Lady, do you refer to Vanessa? I had no idea she was a shaper.'

'Be that as it may, she is and it is imperative she be protected at all times. Go to see The Cybil, I will take you there myself but then you must go and protect Vanessa while Jamie completes his tasks set. I will see you as the sun rises Maeve; now sleep.' Flidais dismissed her.

Maeve hadn't wanted to stay the night, she was keen to get moving, but the traditions of food and a bed was not something a traveller would ever refuse without insulting the host, any more than a Goddess such as Flidais could be.

A young girl met her at the sleeping space, showing her to a bedroll close to the fire pit as if she were an honoured guest. Maeve thanked her, grateful for the fact that everyone else was still awake and by the sound of the music, ready to listen to a tale or two from Bran. She lay on her back listening to the sound of his harp and voice until sleep took her.

She slept soundly until a not too gentle shake woke her. All around the sound of snoring continued as Flidais led her out into the cold morning air; the sun was just rising. Maeve could just make could make out Bran's shape in the gloom. They walked together in silence to the coracle, which would carry them to the Isle.

Raising her arms in invocation, Maeve began the chant she'd learned to call the water sprites but they were already waiting. The coracle moved smoothly across a mirror-still lake. In the quiet of the morning, she could smell the smoke of fires and saw a torch light flickering on the jetty.

When Maeve turned in deference to Flidais to help her out of the coracle, not because she thought the Lady would need it, she realised Flidais was gone.

Bran grinned in the light of the flame, shrugging his shoulders as if to say, 'don't look to me for answers.' Then climbing the ladder, he reached down to pull Maeve up beside him. Leah greeted them enthusiastically before leading them to the hut of The Cybil. To Maeve's surprise, Leah sat down in The Cybil's seat, smiling at Maeve's bemusement.

'You wanted to see me Maeve,' she said directly. 'How can I help you?'

'Well, I came to see The Cybil to find out more about her connection to Sybille and to the Dark Fae, Aelish.'

'I act in the Lady's absence, she is away. Every now and then she goes into retreat and none may interrupt her.'

'Then I have come for nothing,' Maeve said, her mood deflating.

'Well, you haven't asked me anything yet,' Leah smiled gently, reminding Maeve so much of Beth in that moment.

'I didn't think you would know the answer to a question raised about Aelish, but it's this. Who are Aelish's parents?'

'Ah indeed, then you have made a journey for nothing,' Bran made to interject but Leah's raised hand stopped him. 'This is not my story to tell. The Cybil, just as her aspect Sybille must on occasion, goes to renew in the Skeins. Her plan is to find her aspect to see if she can help Sybille. After all this time her physical body will be weak and endangered. The Cybil will but help in the search where she can. As to the parentage of the Lady Aelish that I cannot say.'

Maeve stood up abruptly, forgetting everything she was taught about protocol when dealing with the seers of the Isle. 'I can't believe you won't tell us when it could help us discover why Aelish became dark. We know they are not born so, but that doesn't help us unravel the secrets as to why it happened. Every way we turn there are obstacles put in our path. Will we ever find the right question to ask that will actually give us a straight answer?' She realised at that moment she'd hit the nail on the head. That was it. Everything depended on asking exactly the right question.

'So not completely a wasted journey then?' Leah grinned.

Bran's chuckle followed her as Maeve woke in Max's room in the converted stable at Wells. Jamie, curled at her back, was stroking her arm. She turned into his embrace. 'Are you okay? You were muttering in your sleep and seemed agitated. It sounded as if you were giving someone what for.' He stroked her tangled hair from her face.

'I thought I was really there on the Seer's Isle speaking with Leah. She was sitting in for The Cybil who has gone to find Sybille, her aspect. Leah told me when I asked who Aelish's parents were that she couldn't answer that question but that we had to find the right question in order to finally get a straight answer. Talk about one step forward, three steps back!'

'Well, you did get an answer, just not what you were expecting.'

'Yeah great,' Maeve's muffled oath that followed made him laugh.

'Sleep now. Chances are you were there, walking the Between in your sleep, which makes you more potent than you realise. Dreamwalking is a skill hard to come by, so perhaps this gift of yours may help find Sybille. Let's talk to Rob in the morning but for now, sleep; I'm bushed.' He pulled her closer stroking her hair until he felt her breathing deepen into sleep.

'Thank you Lady Flidais,' he whispered.

'Anything for my Firstborn,' came the reply.

Chapter 25
Stirring

She's stirring now from amidst dead flowers
...quietly she slept through the winter hours
...beneath the stretching wildwood bowers...
Now spring returns and the sweet rain showers
...are washing away the dark

Sybille stirred from a space of deep peace, enveloped in gossamer threads, interwoven with little chiming bells reminiscent of calling birds. Somewhere, there was the sound of a gently throbbing drum. A heartbeat drummed her body, vibrating her senses. What had she been doing before she slept and had, within that sleep, been collapsing, and falling, drifting inwards, downwards?

Stretching, she tried to recall ...why in bed asleep of course! Bed; there was no bed. A cocoon of finely spun silken threads held her. It seemed to move and sway in an unseen breeze. Where was she? Why wasn't she in bed at home where she'd fallen asleep? Where was Morgana? Was she still dreaming? Then why was she so lucid, so aware? If only she could remember. Ah, yes of course, it came in a tide of emotion. She'd been at her desk writing and known that it was her time again to renew.

How she became aware of this was always a mystery and in between was forgotten until the time approached again. Then she would remember, not the details, she would simply disappear and then as suddenly reappear where she had been as if falling asleep. Why did this happen? To replenish the mortal body so that the awful feelings of stretching thinly like wet parchment would abate for another hundred years. Each time she returned to renew, it became more difficult to separate herself from the physical life she lived and the freedom found in knowledge of her real immortal self *'Kanto'noldo,'* her Trueshape, Silver.

Afterwards, all was lost again in the ties and tides of natural lives. So many people thought it would be wonderful for things to stay forever unchanging, forever young of face. If only they knew the pain of seeing loved ones move on to transition and having to fill the days with what was still to do, to experience, in order to help others wake up and remember.

In truth no one really dies, only the personality - created for a short leg of a long journey, sloughed off like a discarded overcoat. Life continued with a different body, a different face. Few realised that it was not just one life at a time but multiple lives, all threads in the continuum of eternal now ...then she was drifting again.

This time Sybille sensed something was very different though ...before plunging deeper into the sleep of renewal, awakening later to find herself curled within a tree; Makers flocked, trying to bring her to her senses.

Drifting, floating, released from the pull of gravity and the weight of the physical body, Sybille saw two women coming towards her, one she thought she knew, the other not.

It was like looking through a mist, a cloud. She thought she *should* know them. She wanted to cry out, but there were no words only images and a strange detachment, as if this were all she was, all she knew, this wraithlike creature - but she had a life, a physical body somewhere. What had happened?

She felt a tug as a gentle voice called to her, but she didn't have the will to find out where the voice came from. She drifted off again into the forest and there, far away in the mists, was an outline, a shadow, of an immense tree.

Floating towards it, she saw tiny, winged beings working to stem the flow of sap oozing from its skin. She knew she should be worried, but the emotion barely registered. Instead, she drifted upwards looking for a resting place in its boughs.

Tired, so tired. Finding a small hollow in its vast trunk, she slipped inside; 'Sleep,' she thought, 'if I rest then I'll remember.'

Chapter 26
...and stirring

I vibrate ...in colour sound and rhythm growing
...when sung, each note is spun
...to shine, awakening within my deepest knowing.

Stretching out with her awareness, Silver sensed the many threads unravelling ...becoming a frayed fabric of memories, lost in the Skeins of Tyme.

How long had she held the threads of this tapestry together? How long would it take to weave them into some semblance of their Trueshape again? Would it happen or would she drift further and further into the outer-reaches of the cosmos, forever floating into forgetfulness, no longer aware of the turning wheel of human lives and loves that she'd experienced through all her myriad Littleshapes?

Something was amiss, she'd never felt this weak, this fragmented, as the dark blight bit into her; she placed a veil over the oozing wound in her belly, soothing the agitated movements of the Makers as something cast a shadow across the soft nest. A Maker hovered at the entrance to the yet unfinished cocoon, but something was wrong; it appeared to be in some distress, its brilliant light was flickering erratically and it changed form constantly, as if searching for a shape to answer the riddle of its existence.

Silver felt her Littleshape Sybille stir from her dreaming to surface again. Sybille emerged from sleep, gazing with awe at the silken cocoon and beyond, to the huge Tree of Birthing from which they were suspended.

A strange and sickening sense of bi-location caused Sybille to wake up fully. She was here in the silken nest but also elsewhere. Ah, yes she remembered, in the tree from which they hung. Here she was conscious in her etheric body and in the tree, her physical body hiding, intuitively seeking a place to recover.

Silver spoke in her mind, *'Much has happened Sybille, while you have slept but now you are awake, I will tell you what has transpired.'*

She held Sybille while she told the story of the Maker's fall and how, through the Skeins of Tyme one broken thread was needed to repair the tapestry that interwove all the lives that once were, now were and which would continue in the expanding universal process. She soothed her to sleep with a song as she continued the story…

Sybille dreamed she was travelling through the great Birthing Tree in which she slept, down inside the branches, the trunk and down into the root system. She was weak, fragile and just wanted to sleep forever.

No longer having a great sense of who or what she was, she floated wraith-like, downwards into the darkness beckoning to her that spoke of relief from all disillusion and fear. From deep within that darkness, a light flickered far away in the depths *'…follow,'* Silver's voice spoke to her, *'follow and then you can rest.'*

Suddenly she was speeding down a great tunnel towards the brightest of lights; hurtling along at an ever-increasing speed until she flew into it …and then she was floating, bathed in a gentle light of restoration and peace. In what seemed only moments, she was waking in a room filled with streaming sunlight on a canopied bed hung with soft white, translucent drapes. Resting against chambray pillows with lace-worked edging, fragrant with fresh rose water. She stretched, smiling to herself as she looked at her firm, olive toned skin with pleasure and yet something niggled at the back of her mind '…young skin,' she thought; 'of course young skin I'm only seventeen after all, aren't I? No,' she thought, 'that's not right, I'm older, surely.'

She stirred again and Silver soothed her with a touch, singing the story as it had unfolded and unfolded still… *Jamie brought Nina to the cottage in the forest beyond Glastonbury and another story began to write itself. Finally, after Magdalena's death, Nina too passed into the Skeins but in her frail being she held the source of all the searching, which then merged within Vanessa Savage, Annie's daughter to Harry Jenkins.*

Silver showed Sybille how the events occurred as Nina passed from the thread Between and from all the other threads of which she'd been a part, to join with her aspect Vanessa, relaying the images and sounds to her through her song… *Makers flocked to Nina as she collapsed to the floor. With their focus only for Nina now, even Nangini did*

Vanessa woke, disentangling herself from sheets, clammy with cold sweat despite the warm night; temperatures soared, post Litha. Staggering out of bed, she walked to the window; the room seemed airless. Cries echoed in her mind and empathic pain ripped through her heart as she felt Nina's struggle for breath, although she knew, in that brief moment of struggle, Nina had finally lost the battle and was gone from the world of man.

Vanessa sank to her knees. She tried to call for help but made no noise beyond the sound of the tortured sobs wracking her body. Her bedroom door flew open as Bethan rushed in; she'd heard her silent scream and came in Arianwen's shape to help.

Light filled the room and a procession of Fae and sprites, moving sedately through the corridors of the Between, approached. Arianrhod, Lunar Goddess of the Wheel, walked in their midst carrying a frail flickering globe of silvery light. She nodded in acknowledgement as Arianwen bowed and left the room.

Arianrhod approached Vanessa, lifting her chin and with a gentle hand, held the glowing sphere of light out to her. *'Nina is gone,'* she sang. *'We could not foresee the Magicks worked by the elder Wytch, La Stregga and Nina's father, Eduard Giraldi, who attempted to prolong a life al-*

ready spent. Who planted this idea in his mind, we cannot know. The Great Mother holds surprises not reckoned with, as we walk in separation from Her. Called on as individuals by humankin when they ask the right question and have the correct motivation, we must act to assist, while they grow through the same illusion of separation from Her. We must endure as the resulting reaction ripples throughout the Web of Ungwe. We will send her physical shell to Eduard that he may grieve her passing from this world; perhaps it will teach him not to meddle with life for his own selfish ends. Aerandir has also learned much from this sweet child.'

'Now,' Arianrhod continued, *'brave woman-child, are you ready to receive Nina's essence, to merge her memories and skills with your own? She is your aspect but slipped away before the merging could occur. We do not ask this lightly of you, rest assured.'*

Vanessa managed to whisper, without hesitation, that she was willing. She looked deep within The Lady's eyes; it was like drowning in a symphony that lifted several octaves in pitch as Arianrhod placed the glowing sphere within Vanessa's open and clean solar plexus centre. She gasped in surprise as Nina's essence merged with her own, expanding her understanding of the nature of the Way. Nina's memories flooded over Vanessa as gently as the young woman had been gentle. No smear of negativity, no dark thoughts or deeds; in fact a life purely and innocently lived. Within the core of Nina's light, Vanessa sensed another note, not of Nina and yet it was and now, of her too. She raised her eyes again to Arianrhod in hope and heard, *'Shhh, little one, no one must know this yet; it must unfold as it will. Do you understand this? We need to appear ignorant of knowing so the one behind all of these events and the results ensuing, not be aware. That way, we may well be able to trace the energy of the perpetrator.'*

'But ...,' Vanessa tried to speak, but The Lady sealed her lips with a gentle finger and a shake of the head. *'There is one other who knows this and he too has been sworn to silence. At least you will know when the time comes, you are not alone but you must wait for the sign I will give you.'* Arianrhod sent an image to Vanessa that she recognised, the same one she had seen on the stone Bethan carried with her everywhere. 'Does Arianwen... Bethan, know?'

'She does as her Trueshape, but as she explained to you all, there is a natural inability to speak until full truth is known and has become wisdom.' With that said she stroked Vanessa's face. Bidding the Fae to come forward, she directed them to lay Vanessa on the bed, casting her into a deep and dreamless sleep that she may meet with Nina again a last time in the physical world.

Sybille slept and while she dreamed, the Makers tended her body, fighting off the Dark Makers with renewed energy. Then another came, one who bore her face, who spoke to her gently of renewal and for her to remember the Seer's Isle. The Cybil finally managed to dribble just a few drops of precious elixir from the Birthing Tree between Sybille's parched lips.

As Vanessa walked the Between, the box holding Sybille's Book of Shadows strapped to her chest, she felt a strange stirring in her belly. 'Nina?' she said quietly.

'No, she is here but no, I am not Nina.'

Once again, Sybille moved restlessly in sleep, as the Makers sang of recovery.

Chapter 27
Beth and Leah Remember

...She's stirring now feel her push on your soul
...giving life, renewing, birthing everything that's whole
...deep in the forests He's running unseen
...soon they will wed and give birth to the green

 Leah sat; a small journey harp lay idle in her lap. Bran the Cunningman had begun to teach her the Bardic rhythms of poetry and song and she was straining to focus on a piece that had been haunting her for a while. It wasn't anything he'd shown her. It was lilting and as wistful as turnings seasons can be.

She could sense her Beth aspect from the other thread in the Skeins and had been glad to hear that little Alma had finally found a home. Concern had filled her for the child when she'd collected her from the lakeside, a few summers ago now. Alma had been a wee thing and had struggled with the thought that the only parents she seemed to remember had sold her to the Priestess of the Seer's Isle. So much had occurred since and little Alma had died on the thread woven by the Lady and been re-born, according to Arianwen, to reunite with Maeve. Maeve too she remembered; her pain had driven her to madness and they feared for her life. She was sent to

Scathach's hearth; such was her wilfulness and there, been reunited, on a different thread, with Alma.

Leah remembered another time when the Great Rite of Beltane was enacted by The Cybil and The Merlyn of the Forests, resulting in a different child. She'd been but a novice child herself and knew nothing much of her own parentage, so she'd felt for the resulting child of that union; had been close at the hour of her birth. Fetching water for the Elder Midwife, she'd seen the strange changeling child that had made even The Cybil recoil.

Leah made the warding sign automatically as she remembered that night, before reaching again for her harp. She felt Beth start with surprise at the images her meanderings had conveyed to her aspect. A dark wytchling child that should not have come of such a sacred union, particularly when it may well be a Priestess of the Isle one day but the Great Mother sent universal messages of pleasure or displeasure according to her will. Mostly, this will was entirely unforseen and unfathomable, even by the seers.

Straining to remember the haunting song, she returned her focus to her music, hoping it might please the Cunningman, an oft surly teacher.

Listening intently, she heard a deep male voice but it wasn't Bran's; this one had richer tones not of this thread, she thought. Perhaps the Fae were visiting tonight, so close to Beltane as the wheel turned again.

With a rustle of great wings, a massive raven landed on the rock next to her. She knew the changers well, especially Tara and Rowan but this was a stranger to her eyes.

He's comely she thought, a light blush colouring her cheeks as he changed, naked and unabashed in front of her; coiling tattoos wound down one side of his face, neck and shoulder, from hairline to his long tapering musician's fingers. He spoke with a strange sounding brogue that she had to concentrate to understand, not wishing to appear rude and not quite sure where to look.

He smiled a smile that didn't quite reach his eyes, which held the wisdom of ages. Her healer strengths came to the surface, replacing any misgivings about being alone on the edge of the forest without attendants. She'd escaped them; her training was hard and long; sometimes she just needed space and solace to be who she was, not who she was supposed to be becoming.

'May I,' he indicated the little harp she held.

'Why, yes.' She passed it to him, not even wondering why; the timbre of his voice perhaps with his lilting accent, which she recognised was from across the border into the Wildlands where the woad people lived. Sometimes they encroached here but were never violent toward the people of the Isle, bringing offerings of dye and pungent tasting vegetables she couldn't identify. They were also metalworkers and forged wonderful simple metal tools and chalices from the ore in the mines that they worked. Fierce though they were, they were also peace loving. How had this shaper gained their brogue? He was far too large to be one of them. He took the harp from her unprotesting fingers and began to sing the very tune she'd been trying to catch and hold.

'It's called Circle Dance. Beth …erm Arianwen?' Leah nodded her understanding, 'and I, wrote it. I'd be happy to teach you in return for a little information.'

'If I have knowledge of what you seek, it's yours,' Leah smiled openly, reminding him fondly of Beth.

Morgan sang…

'She changes her gown, as the year grows old from russet to amber …green to gold. She's the Lady of the harvest for all living things, in the hedgerows and forests a rich bounty She brings.

He changes His cloak as She changes Her gown; they dance at Lammas' hay wain, 'til in sacrifice He's cut down.

Yet they dance on and on as the falling leaves twirl …through the mossy glades twilight to the pipes sobbing skirl that breaks through the silence of a darkening year …then on toward Mabon, the crisp air becomes clear.

On they dance toward Samhain, the ancestors awake …the Wild Hunt comes riding the years' fallen to take. Through the veil brightly gleaming, long hair darkly streaming …and the hound's wild belling, cause the forests to shake.

On and on yet they dance to Yule's last long dark day …the light becomes stronger, yet Jack Frost's still at play …but on they dance toward Imbolc as the first lambs are born, …ever onward to bright Ostara, the sun's rays become warm.

Then when May blossoms open, their honey perfumes the air …step abroad as the sun rises to make a wreath for your hair …for here at the rite of Beltane their dance flames with bright joy …and folk may later harvest …a girl or a boy.'

Leah blushed again and laughed aloud at the last line; Morgan grinned in return.

'On to Litha they dance, sweet berries flavour the wine …the sun's power reaches zenith and will slowly decline. On the breeze, you'll hear Her singing … in the thunder His rumbling mirth …when they call us, we'll dance with them …in circle spinning …death to rebirth.'

Leah listened absorbed in variations she'd not come across before. Lending her high, reedy voice to his deep baritone, she sang it through again with him, hoping she would remember the complex chords he played.

As soon as they'd finished Morgan sobered again. 'I'm sorry, I should introduce myself. I am not of this thread but am close friends with your aspect and I am an aspect of Bran, just as you are of Beth.' He hesitated a moment considering his choice of words. 'Do you know of the Ravenkin Rowan?' he asked directly.

'I do,' Leah replied without pause. 'She was often here but then she suddenly disappeared and we were told she fell from this thread, which shapers never do unless there has been a great abuse of power by something or someone. There were whispers of a curse,' she almost whispered. Without turning her head, she indicated with her eyes they were no longer alone.

Morgan blinked and nodded almost imperceptibly as his eyes looked beyond her to the forest edge. He tensed; he knew who stood there and knew there was no time to lose. 'When did this happen; when did she disappear?' command in his voice.

'Why several moon passages past,' Leah replied unerringly.

'Can you lead me there to the place she was last seen?'

'Yes, it's not far from Scathach's Hearth, but what of the watcher?' she lowered her tone, lest it carry on the breeze to the silent entity.

'She will follow but this is exactly what I want. Are you able to take me when the moon is at its closest to the moment she left?'

'That would be in just a day or so but the season is wrong. It was Samhain when she left apparently.'

'No matter,' he replied gently, sensing her agitation; her eyes flitted to where she knew the watcher stood. 'If I come back when the moon is just right in the sky, it would be Beltane again, yes?

'Yes, indeed the Great Rite is come again.' She smiled, wishing for once she was not a priestess bound by vows, but knowing he was not for her.

Morgan quickly told her the same story she knew from Bethan of their friend Sam, closely tied to the Ravenshaper Rowan. Leah knew Sam-Rowan had taken his heart, even if he didn't.

'Then meet me here the day the moon next rises full and I will take you there.'

'Just at dusk before it rises,' said Morgan, 'and thank you for your help. You have no idea what this means to many waiting, not just for Rowan's return but also for her Aunt Sybille, missing many winters now; The Cybil is her aspect.'

'Then this could change the threads of the Skeins,' Leah frowned in concentration and a little fear. 'I have seen much to fear. Once when the one known as Maeve lost her wee friend Alma and on another thread when she lost her mind with grief for the same child stolen by a Dark Fae; she set fire to the Isle in her grief, poor woman. All this is potential, all threads must be regathered or they will be more than that; they will entangle the Skeins of Tyme. I fear for all who walk your journey with you, Morgan,' she pronounced it Mor-han. 'There are still trials to face for all of you who have come together to do the impossible.' Her eyes had glazed over, white's showing, before she recovered herself, sipping from a small flask at her side. She took another small clay bottle out of her pouch, handing it to Morgan. 'Here, you may need this for your lady,'

Morgan's eyes darkened at her words as they hit home. 'Beth had the bracelet I see and now you would return it to its owner, no doubt?' She smiled at him before gathering her little harp, placing it gently in its cover. 'Farewell, Morgan Ravenshaper, until the next full moon rises.'

He touched her hand with respect and shifted shape in a heartbeat.

On another thread, Beth stopped what she was doing, reaching out with all her newly developed senses; 'Morgan,' she laughed with delight, running to share with the others. 'Morgan's coming home.' No one doubted the truth of her words.

Chapter 28
Beyond the Dreaming Spirits

She's stirring now feel her push on your soul
...giving life, renewing, birthing everything that's whole
Deep in the forests He's running unseen
...soon they will wed and give birth to the green

On reaching Greenman Ways, the group piled into two cars and drove to the farm where Robyn waited. He looked at Vanessa strangely, backing away from her as she went to hug him.

'What in the name of all names are you carrying, child? It smells of heat and metal.'

'Oh, sorry Robyn, I've not told anyone yet. I wanted to get it through the veil before showing it to anyone or worse, Aelish discovering it.'

Robyn kept his distance but smiled at her. 'Okay, let's go round the back. You can't bring the box into the house, only the contents.'

As the group arrived no banter or laughter relieved the tense atmosphere. This was it; time to finish the job. No matter how it turned out they wouldn't say they hadn't tried.

Vanessa put the bag on the table in the garden, away from the house. She pulled out the heavy metal box and opening it, took out a large, cloth wrapped item. Gathering round the friends knew instantly what it was just by its shape and by the aroma that rose from the cloth.

'Sybille's book,' Beth laughed aloud. 'You clever girl. Where was it?'

'Well I can't take credit for it. It was Da... Harry who left it for me, along with this note. Is everyone here? I'll read it then...

Vanessa,

There are no words, only hopes of one day hearing that you forgive me. I knew nothing of your birth; your mum kept you hidden from everyone but now, perhaps we will all learn why, as the web unravels. Perhaps, her friendship with Claire eventually outweighed the affair she and I had. At the end of the day, Aelish's glamour hooked me in, in the first place and even when over would not let me go. I'm not proud of it, weak male that I am, I do not like what I became.

Anyway, somehow, your mum's looking after me now. I felt her with me and heard her whispering; I even felt her hand on my cheek. I will be changed Vanessa and in time I hope I may get to know you. I am not a bad man, just a weak one and I'm paying the price for everything with as much courage as I can muster. Therefore, I leave no address that I may keep you safe, for you to do what is ordained you do and then, when it's all done, perhaps I may get to know you, finally.

Please tell Claire that I remember now why I first loved her and Flora; she is the child I dreamed of who achieved all the things I was too cowardly to do.

With deep regret and growing respect,

Harry.'

Silence was a palpable, living thing as she finished, looking round at their faces. Written there she saw sorrow, pain, surprise, disbelief and in Claire's eyes, relief. At that moment, she felt a weight lift and Pwyll stepped forward to take her hand.

'Do you understand now Naboo?' he whispered.

'Yes,' Claire said firmly. 'Just another weak male and obviously it doesn't matter whether they be human or changer.' She pulled away. 'I understand Pwyll but I need a little time to digest this because I've blamed Harry instead of seeing the glamour Aelish had him under, through Annie's 'alter ego.' Still that said; this is not the time to be thinking of our personal issues, there are far greater things at stake.' Turning to Vanessa, she said, 'Thank you Nessa, for sharing the message and although we may not know where Harry has gone, he'll be back when he's done what he has to do.' She hugged Vanessa and then Flora. 'Looks like I have two daughters then.' They smiled through their tears.

Vanessa opened the wrappings from around the package to reveal Sybille's Book of Shadows. With a joint sigh of relief, they all hugged Vanessa and then each other.

'Now,' said Cal, 'let's get to work!'

They moved inside with the book and their bags of meagre belongings. As always, Robyn had food out to keep their bodies fed and a strong brew of herbal tea to keep them sharp and aware.

Flo spread the bags of herbs on the table with the Grimoire; Cal helped pull out the labelled packets they'd sorted from the hundreds of herb varieties. Vanessa sat the beautifully made Book of Shadows on the table and as she did, parchment sheets fell out, covered in the same scratchy markings as the Grimoire and herb labels. 'Robyn?' Nessa handed him the sheet.

He read the first page through carefully before sharing the contents…

'*Merry Meet, I am the one known as Silver. I am the one who will whisper in your ear as I share a story of mystery and Magicks of which you may be unaware. I will be there as you turn these pages, leaning over your shoulder as you read. You may not know I am there but you may feel my breath upon your cheek, although told this is very rude. I observe your body language change; your facial expressions give so much away. Mirth …scorn …doubt …fear! It's really all the same to me for after all you're the one finding this book, these sheets and choosing to read them, which indeed, has been long in the cauldron of creation. I have coaxed and cajoled Sybille into putting pen to paper or fingers to keyboard but here 'tis and together we will tell you our story of discovery for we are one in truth. So let us begin at the beginning; for that is where I assume we must in order not to confuse, as I am often wont to do in my ramblings! I am my humankin Sybille's Trueshape. I am her continuing self after the Littleshapes fall away into physical decay - like feathers falling from a bird's wing or petals from a flower. I say physical with good reason for the Littleshapes journey on unless they doubt and then, I, Silver, shall diminish a little.'*

The second sheet caused Robyn to scowl. He looked at each of them as they stood transfixed. 'Come on everyone sit down; make yourselves comfortable. This may take some time.' They settled and he continued reading read to them...

Sybille's Teachings: Trueshapers

Beyond the light of dreaming stars
...beyond the light of time
...I reached within to find a space
...a place that's only mine.
A place of light and healing sound
...the darkness was its source
...for from that darkness light was born
...and matter its resource

A Trueshaper is the greater aspect (over-soul) of all the combined aspects of an individual, (new agers call it soul-self) and they in turn are an aspect of the highest ideals; Goddess or God-self if you will as of course, even Deity is one in Primordial Source. Each of the aspects of a concurrent life, (as you know everything is now), are known as Littleshapes, sparks of life-essence that fly between lives, animating the physical body and creating the lessons and experiences of the individual's journey.

At present in this realm, the journeying is unconscious for most and most believe, if they believe at all, that time is linear and that they must die first before they can have an understanding of other lives, other aspects of self, known as sleepers, innocents or Onceborn.

Our job when we awaken is to protect them, for they are not bad, even when their fearful behaviour causes them to do dreadful, destructive things to themselves and each other. They are innocent to the extent of their true selves and therefore need to awaken, each in their own time and yet, every so often, we reach what may be described as a critical mass in our planetary evolution, which pushes us inwardly toward change; these are the moments of opportunity for spiritual growth that can awaken a sleeper. We are at such a moment now in our history.

We understand our challenges better when we know these things, for even the White Christ of the Christian peoples said, 'They know not what they do.' Eastern philosophies speak of Karma and this of course is a version of what I have outlined but still perceives time to be a linear process from past to present and on into an unknown, 'fated' future.

This is a fabricated concept, for life and the universe do not understand the meaning of the invention of the clock and man has looked to understand time by attempting to harness it, which in turn limits understanding of alternative concepts. Of course, we see the sun rise and set, the length of a day and night, a lunar or solar cycle, etcetera yet, under the laws of the universe, this is but an illusion. We would probably go insane if we were to attempt to grasp the entirety of the known and unknown worlds, all happening at the same time and ourselves as vast, eternal beings, miniscule parts, cells of

*our many selves, vibrating; animating our aspects in contin-
uum.*

*If we can see it rather more as a tapestry of threads, each
thread a separate life, and yet one thread in the tapestry links
each life, one to the other. Not just our own journey but also
everyone's journey; through this our understanding of the
process is broadened, becoming less insular. We can then 'jig-
gle' one of those threads from our current life perspective,
drawing to us the knowledge our other aspects have collected,
to assemble a body of knowledge that may become 'whole' to
itself.*

*Is this how a new philosophy is born, perhaps? If we
have a particular skill we are successful at but have no formal
or even fleeting training in this consciousness, chances are we
have brought this quality with us or are remembering what
we achieved in another aspect of ourselves*

*In turn, we can glean information from these other as-
pects of self as we link with them in consciousness. In reverse,
when we feel confronted by characteristics we will not own as
our own; those that are negative, spontaneous outbursts of
violent behaviour, for instance, this may well be where ancestral memory strands overlap; we must not use this as an excuse to make our behaviour okay, however. I have seen many
who would blame their 'other lives' as an excuse for their bad
behaviour. Seen them use it as a crutch, instead of something
to work through or integrate within, much as people with
addictive traits must do. They know it is a part of them to
monitor until they find the origin. It is also advisable to realise that the goal is not perfection in the individual aspect, per*

se but rather in the True-shape acquiring knowledge, through all the countless possibilities, within multiple and concurrent lives; and this is the desired outcome to all our meanderings

We may liken this to something that is rare on this planet, other than in sporting teams and in some families or tribes, namely 'teamwork'.

There are theories today that promise separation from ancestral and cellular memory in this life and that would be valid if we were to see beings who were in fact the equivalent of the White Christ, The Magdalena, Brighid, Buddha, Mohammed, Cerridwen, Hecate and other such worthy beings who have walked this realm. But what happened to them?

In other words we have to actually know (or at least have some idea) where we are going, when we hear speak of 'ascension' (although this alludes to a hierarchy or an escape route) to other planes or we may indeed become lost in the 'Between'. Therefore, we may consider finding/creating a place that becomes so real to us on the inner; we then manifest it as the place that becomes where we will go (rather than where a hierarchy tells us we will, scaring us or wooing us with pleasure).

Is this another aspect or a final coming together of all aspects? That is, of course, up to you to decide! When we understand this all egocentric agendas fall away, we know we do not die but merely change form, our essence remains the same yet grows, as we gather all the aspects of self into one being, which is united in consciousness and without fear, for fear is egocentric and is the controller. Fear is the self that *believes having things, accumulating assets, will make the ego-self happy and keep them safe.*

Fear has created hierarchical orders, including wealthy and poor, weak and strong, religious right and wrong in a judgemental manner. Sadly, the wealth associated with the accumulation of things, cannot sustain or indeed be eaten when one is starving.

Like little ratchets in a finely tuned clock, cogs spun and understanding chimed. Everything Sybille had ever taught was here in her book; now to find the relevant words to match the herbs, tools and anything else they could pull together from their joint understanding.

'Right,' said Cal, 'where is the place you believe you will go when you reach the end of this thread? How does it link all your aspects together and what is the meeting point for all those aspects or at least the relevant ones recently discovered; those with a role or link to Sybille and all that's gone down?'

Robyn handed out pens and notepaper.

Beth stood, pacing a few steps before turning to face them all. 'The thread that links, not just me but all of us, is Sybille on the one hand and Aelish on the other; personally for me it's Leah, so where do these actually connect? Any idea, Robyn?'

To everyone's surprise, he looked at the floor, all appearance of the wise sage and earth spirit gone. He looked like a defeated and sad old man.

Alma sidled up to him; gone was the child, gone even the Merrow as her face aged, becoming stern and wise for an instant before she took his hand, her little face returning to wide-eyed innocence. 'Tell the story Robert Cromlech.'

'No, you know all about me you need to know. Would you speak so to Lord Hercurin?' he said as his horn tips protruded briefly. Even this was not as they remembered at the last Rite when he'd revealed his identity.

'Without doubt,' she retorted sharply. 'For these friends I would do anything, I am no longer frightened. Aelish's misdirected power cannot harm me anymore.'

The watching group held their breath as they waited to see how Robyn would respond but his horns disappeared and his face relaxed back into the familiar gentle features.

'What are you hiding?' Lily asked him directly. 'Don't we have enough secrets standing in the way of finding Sybille, who you purport to have known for so long?'

'Lily,' Beth warned her gently, her face and hair shimmering with unusually threatening energy. 'You know I know, Robyn, you know I have seen both you and Pwyll as The Cybil's High Priest at seasonal rites. At first, I thought it was Sybille but it was interchangeable; recently with Sybille and earlier on, with The Cybil on a long ago thread, when the Seer's Isle was visible for anyone with eyes to see. Why did it disappear? What did you do, you and The Cybil? When did you become her High Priest and when did you see me on the aether as I was called time and again to your Rites?'

'Yes,' said Cal, 'you showed your face to us at the Yule Rite and told us what we wanted to hear, but was it everything?'

Without hesitation, he shaped to his Robyn form but not the Robyn Goodfellow, friendly, woodland sprite who held the balance of the land between the cycles for the Lord of Nature. He wasn't laughing and had grown tall and stately, much as Hercurin did. He sported small horns, which were growing to full antlers. In the British Isles he was the Spirit of the Land of Albion along with his Lord, Herne the Hunter. He held the promise of spring's return and in autumn, an abundant wine harvest.

'You said you were Sybille's lover. Were you also The Cybil's?' Beth queried.

'Yes, I was Sybille's lover and her friend, as I told you before,' he replied simply, 'and still am; I only wait her return from renewal and I know this will happen. We are twin souls; that is to say one soul living in two physical bodies on the same thread.' He continued to tell the story of the Birthing Tree, referring back to Sybille's text in her Book of Shadows and the renewal of souls, willingly con-scious, who go beyond the single identity of their ego per-sona, embracing all aspects of self until they became uni-fied, whole. Sybille is the aspect Silver has waited for and Silver is as much Sybille, as Sybille is Silver. They blinked in unison at his words, trying to understand the nature of such a consciousness.'

'You would know, Bethy and most of you here... you've all found those aspects and bonded with them. They still exist where their threads wind through the Skeins, just as you continue on here. When you become fully conscious, cease to fight the larger portion of you, which is pure spirit, you will understand that there are multiple aspects roaming through the web of Ungwe both conscious and unconscious of your existence too. It's not only here on this earth thread we lose our way; there are many ways we can go astray,' he glanced at each in turn.

'It would be so much simpler if we could just be re-minded of this when we fall into unconsciousness,' said Vanessa, knowing she'd experienced all of this before.

'You didn't answer the question,' said Maeve, iron in her tone as she waited for Robyn's reply.

'Well?' Jamie questioned.

Robyn refused to reply. In silence, one by one they began collecting their things together. There would be no help forthcoming here they thought, their hearts sinking. A door slammed somewhere in the house and then with a crash Tara almost fell through the door.

'Tell them you old goat!' she screamed at Rob. 'Enough of the games, you have no reason not to tell them or I will.'

Beth moved to stand beside Tara, Aerandir stood in the doorway. 'We are firstborn,' he said. 'Along with the shapers, we are the Firstborn of Danu. Will you hold out longer Robyn Goodfellow or will you tell us the truth. Will we call the Lady to intervene? What do you think Sybille would want?' These were the magic words as Rob took a sharp intake of breath.

'Yes!' he muttered an oath. 'The Cybil and I were lovers. Sybille and The Cybil are but different aspects of the same Trueshape as you well know.'

'What else?' A deep voice came from the open doorway. Morgan, touching Aerandir on the shoulder in a brief greeting, stepped in. No one moved although Lily longed to throw herself at him with sheer joy.

'We had a child, a product of the Great Rite. Sybille wasn't able to have a child on this thread, so I returned to the thread we shared, where her aspect and I co-joined, Priest and Priestess together. At the Beltane Rite, we conceived a girl child but something was not as it should be. She was a strange creature and we feared she would corrupt the other Priestesses on the Seer's Isle. By thirteen she was a strangely sexual being for a child who appeared Elven, although her Firstborn blood through me gave her the similarity of facial structure. We sent her to the Elven Elders when she began to show the tendency toward Dark Fae; wild elemental spirits whom, not necessarily bad, are volatile, unpredictable, so we contrived she be Aithlin's sister and the Elders agreed, for their own reasons no doubt.

Aithlin's father had gone into the west and his mother was frail after he did; they shared themselves at the deepest level of Elven understanding. No one knew, only guessed, Aelish was the product of a fling with a wildling. Only a handful knew the truth and we kept it even from Aelish.

As Alma rightly corrected us, she wasn't always Dark Fae. They are not born, rather creating themselves through their own negative and unsavoury needs. The Cybil and I never imagined something so twisted would come from our union.

Aelish must have known for a long time who her parents were. How she discovered it is a mystery but from that moment on, she was determined to wreak havoc wherever our threads crossed and any other soul who, unaware, crossed our paths, particularly Firstborn shifters of any shape or creed.'

'And what of Sam,' Morgan's voice held impatience, all respect he'd felt was tinged with anger at the twisted stories unfolding. It remained for him to tell his story but they were all so shocked by the tale Rob told they were content to hug Morgan and wait for him to be ready to share where he had been.

'As you know, Morgan,' Rob continued, 'Sam was caught in a nasty relationship with her parents. Her ability to see had brought her trouble on many occasions as a child. Sybille saw her sister's girl showing signs of possessing abilities that were more unusual, handed down through their ancient lineage. Sybille knew this would make things difficult for all involved. Her sister, never understanding the Way, became involved with a man, married him and into his strange cult.

The dogma prescribed anything unusual to be a sign that a person who witnessed visions was either mad or possessed. That is, unless they were the cult leader, of course.

Sybille had no control over the upbringing of Samantha but was concerned that the girl was becoming withdrawn and apathetic due to the 'treatments',' Rob scribed parenthesis in the air, 'her parents took her to. At least soon, we thought Sam would be able to make decisions for herself. When she broke away and went to live on campus as she'd planned, Sybille only hoped it would not be too late, the damage done. What lay dormant in Sam was truly amazing, but how to tell the girl, with Tara so resistant… well that's another story.'

'No, continue now,' Tara barked.

Rob sighed, he knew he could pull rank but these brave kin demanded answers and he was growing tired, needing his counterpart to come home was all he could think of.

He continued, 'Samantha came to stay with Sybille when her parents went away on their travels to 'Holy sites'. At first, Sam was reticent to speak to Sybille about her parents, loyal to a fault but Sybille could see she needed a listening ear and was shocked to hear of the control her father required over her every move; it was not healthy and it was easy to see Sam was brewing to rebel.

Sybille made her aware she always had a place to come to at the farm in Covenstead and she came to the Sabbats and Esbats, if only as a way to escape from home for a weekend in the country; she was the daughter we never had on this thread.' Morgan's eyes narrowed at his words.

'Only on this thread?' he queried, his tone tinged with irony, exchanging looks with Beth, whose eyes widened at his inference.

Rob ignoring him, continued. 'Sybille loved to see Sam relax a little, wandering the gardens with her sketchbook, drawing to her hearts' content; another thing her parents said was a waste of time. Sam grew and finally stood up to them. She said she was considering journalism, after her first year studying law, which was her father's idea for her future. Sam was bright; she left school early, ahead of her classmates and went to Uni. She changed course mid-stream, unable to comply any longer with her father's wishes; the rest you know from what she told you, after Tara used hypnosis and you,' he turned to Tara, 'are just as responsible for hiding details from Samantha about her ancestry and her gifts.'

'Did no one think Sam had the courage and enough ability if properly trained, to accept her role just as any of us here have had too?' Vanessa spoke up.

'She became a rebel, not wanting to know anything after her gifts that were blocked,' said Tara. 'You'll all remember how tetchy she was and how you were worried about how she'd react with Sybille gone. As you know it was the making of her.'

'All the more reason to have reversed the hypnosis sooner, don't you think?' Maeve interjected harshly.

Quietly to himself, as he guided them through the journey, telling just enough to keep them thinking and acting forcefully, Rob thought how magnificent they were to stand up to a Forestlord, a united front. This was exactly what Tara and he had intended with their little display; they exchanged a triumphant glance.

'Did you know of this, Pwyll?' Claire dared him with her eyes to lie.

'No I did not,' he replied.

Not satisfied however and seeing the look Tara and Rob had exchanged, Beth rose from where she sat. 'Why was this held back from us and do you both realise we're not fools?' She turned to the group taking Morgan's hand in her own. 'So, I think we need to hear where Mor's been, I've had enough of the games for one night. At least I know he'll tell us the truth without embellishment, over or understatement. We'd planned to spend the night here and some time to get the rites written for Mabon. We agreed to split into two groups to perform the Mabon and Ostara rites at the same time in both hemispheres but now, frankly I don't know what to think.'

'We're all tired Bethy, let's leave everything to the morning and start afresh,' Flo spoke up for the first time. 'Mor's dead on his feet and needs to rest. What he has to share he can share tomorrow, because it doesn't look to me as if he could bring Sam back.'

'It's a long story,' said Morgan, 'and yes I'm wiped out by it all but at least let me say Sam is alive but the conditions to bring her home are complicated and how we handle the rites needs to be looked at as if we were performing delicate surgery. Otherwise Sam and Sybille may be lost to us for good.' With that, Morgan's legs went from under him, Cal and Jamie caught him before he hit the floor. Between them, they carried him to the couch; Lily and Pwyll sat with him, talking quietly, while he slept, happy he was back safely.

Spreading themselves through the rambling old farmhouse, they each found a place to curl up until morning. Max went home to feed Honey and Beth went home, hoping Morgan's news would put a new light on things.

Hidden in the silk wrap, the precious shard attached to the oak shaft vibrated in song. Alma and Beth heard it with a sigh of relief as they exchanged glances with Vanessa, who smiled in acknowledgement. Morgan realised he could understand every word the music he heard spoke to him; even as he slept they entered his consciousness and the delicate silver bangle, hidden in his pocket, thrummed in answer.

On waking, he found Lily sound asleep. He rose to stretch, limbs cramped from scrunching his tall frame in one position on the small couch for so long and was stunned to find an hour had passed since Bethan and Tara left the room.

Finding the bathroom, he splashed cold water over his face. Reaching for a towel, he glanced in the mirror and froze. The sprites had done their work again, twisting portions of his hair into dreadlocks. A fresh raven feather hung from a braid that pulled one side of his heavy fall of hair away from his face, revealing the side of his forehead they'd covered in intricate tattoos of feathers, flames and leaves, which mirrored Sam's exactly. Used to seeing them by now and knowing the shapes and forms well, he stared at the images, which had appeared to change. They writhed on his skin in a dance of sinuous movement, in time to the music he still heard from the silk wrapped object, knowing it as the wand Cal had crafted. Focusing in on the detail, he noted subtle changes, realising the alterations they'd made were telling a story of where he and Sam had been, connected and disconnected throughout the Skeins. What he also saw was a darker journey for Sam yet to come and, inevitably, by him because where Sam went he would follow.

He felt honoured again by the work of the nature sprites that were so loyal to Sam and who were helping him in ways no one else would see unless they were intimate with the designs on his skin. With a sharp intake of breath Morgan straightened, drawing his shoulders back and lifting his head stoically to face what was still to come. At that moment, he shifted from changer-Cunningman to Brandubh Raven warrior, the tattoos on his face adding a maturity and purpose to his striking features.

Chapter 29

Morgan

As we believe, so it is true
...even shape is illusion ...knowledge hidden in you
When you remember ...when you awake
...who will you be ...what is your true shape?
Raven or owl ...fox or blue jay
...each is within ...find the key there today
When you remember ...when you awake
...who are you really ...what is your true shape?
In each cell of your being ...a memory lies
...it's not found in the ethers ...nor in deep blue skies.
When you remember ...when you awake
...who are you truly ...what form will you take?

 Morgan had no time to think, only react, when Sam vanished as if sucked into a vortex. He grabbed the bracelet Beth held out to Sam, vowing he would bring her home. Without the conscious ability to change, she was in trouble and his natural instinct was to follow.

Sam was plummeting hard so he sent his thoughts to her in raven imagery but, caught in the midst of pain and fear, she was deaf to all but the latter, which in itself was the initiator of the unnatural change their amulets prevented.

Pulling together all his strength and being mindful to keep a tight hold on the bracelet he clutched, Morgan shifted shape to fly like an arrow through the aethers, taking no note of where they headed, keeping only Sam in his sights. He was determined that this should be the end of it all; no matter the outcome, he would bring her home; as yet he had failed.

He blacked out on impact and dreamed of moments throughout the last two years, from which he began to piece things together as he drifted in and out of dreams and memories, each held small clues to all the months; years of searching. A melody flitted through his mind as he lay contemplating the canopy of trees and the dappled light that filtered down to reflect on droplets of water on the luscious green foliage. He didn't know where he was and he had no strength to move although he could see Sam lying just a few feet away, her face relaxed, free of pain and he knew she merely slept.

A haunting melody seemed to come from everything around him as if the trees themselves were singing. Words whispered on the breeze and he realised he should feel cold with the amount of moisture on everything, still touched by patches of frosty rime.

I saw a moonraaven flying the night ...her smoky-blue wings full of shadows and light ...and with a silvery twist, my spirit took flight ...chasing moonraaven flying the night.

Then he felt himself flying again with many Ravenkin, a memory he knew because he could still feel his body connected to the earth where he sprawled. 'Perhaps I've broken my back in the fall,' he thought but no signals of alarm rippled through his body, no distress or pain as he shifted consciousness; shifting shape to fly with his Raven friend Ruark across deep, green seas, across an endless red desert, stunted with curious trees and skimming low over a giant red rock. Soaring up and away, above mountains tipped with early snows, his wings responding to the weight of pellucid ice fragments ...then down, down swooping across a valley of green vines and luscious fruits, ready for the harvest. His sensitive, rolled tongue anticipated their sweetness, quenching his thirst in his mind, together with a ripple of danger at the idea of plundering a morsel or two from under the vintner's nose.

Within his Corvidae mind he heard Ruark laugh with glee as she read his senses easily. It would have been just a small thing to be tempted away from the journey for a small respite, but she drove him relentlessly on. With a click of her beak and a guttural call, she winged lower, finding her bearings to land with a clatter of taloned feet onto the roof of an old barn. Sybille's barn he recalled.

He followed, attempting to bank his speed but unaccustomed to the long flight, overshot the roof, sliding down with a snapping of wings to regain equilibrium, hearing a rending tear echoing as he tore through the veil, finally coming to rest at the feet of the towering raven feather-clad being The Morrigan.

He heard laughter and saw there were many other shapers gathered; Pwyll and Claire he recognised instantly and thought he caught sight of Flo in her wren form, a flash of blue as he glimpsed his sister Jay-Lily among the hundreds of tiny birds around them and of course, to the right of their Lady, sat Tara.

Two foxes sat at her feet, Jamie he recognised and with a start, Vanessa, his human mind wondered when this had happened.

The Morrigan spoke to him in the raven tongue, '*Creoso mellonamin, and anta. Amin tel'fallan, hiraeth. Esta sinome.*' 'Welcome my friend, gently now. I can help you if you'll let me.' She reached out her hand and all but lifted him to shaking legs.

'Which thread is this Lady and why am I here. I've not been to a gathering before with the Firstborn.'

'You are a Firstborn Brandubh and have been to many such gatherings but you have slept a while and I have given you time enough to wake up,' she answered him. 'It is here you will gather information you and your friends need to bring Rowan home.'

'Then I thank you Lady. You can count on me.'

'Your loyalty has never been questioned,' she smiled, tugging on a braid of his hair and fastening a feather from her own cape. It smelt of the musky scent of any raven but stronger; so pungent he thought he would pass out in pleasure

He heard laughter from the gathering and then he was away again, this time he walked the narrow, familiar laneways of his countryside, his fierce, dark features screwed up against the brute force of driving rain. He wanted only to be home now with a bowl of hot soup to warm his inner.

He'd played that night at a local pub, accompanying an aspiring young girl, who sang like an angel and looked like a Vampire, the clarity of her voice and the Goth visuals warring with each other as she stood on the stage singing an old song in the traditional Welsh tongue.

She'd looked tired and frail, yet very familiar and he tried to put a memory together as to when he'd met her before. He'd soon discovered, as he played, that she was indeed somewhat like the stories of vampires of old. It wasn't blood she drank though but the energy of his music, which she used to fill herself. At barely 19 in human years, she appeared almost spent; close up her skin was pallid and bore a yellowish tinge.

In that moment, he realised who she was and why he was experiencing these particular moments again, as she latched on to him. He'd just packed up his instruments to leave when small, pale hands clung to his chest; slender fingers, hooked like bird claws bit into his flesh, drawing blood and he watched in fascination as black, spiralling, webbed markings crawled down across his chest to writhe up and down his arm. He remembered when the little leaf sprites had tattooed his face, neck, chest and arm and watched as they came to life now to undo the blight as it writhed toward his heart. He blinked and they were gone. Morgan shook her off, not without compassion for her obvious distressed state. With a curt nod the experience of then and now blended together, giving him the answers he needed to take back with him.

'You'd best be looking after yourself then, Kelly Rush,' he said, hearing a hiss from her, before he strode out into the wet night with a sigh of utter relief but her strident laughter and the words, 'You'll not reject me Brandubh,' followed him clearly over the rain. 'Next time Brandubh, next time.' Her voice held the distinct threat of the Dark Fae Aelish. Was there nowhere she hadn't tainted, he wondered?

'Wales, in early spring, was wet and cold at the best of times but there appeared to be another force behind it tonight,' he thought, as a strange anxiety gripped him. For a moment all was still as if he stood in a small vortex protected from the elements by Goddess knew what; a strange stirring in the trees along the roadside brought him to a halt to listen intently. He was accustomed to strange phenomena but something didn't feel right. He felt agitated, an unusual emotion for him. As he stood, barely touched by the storm, he heard a voice, someone calling him by his Truename. A name he thought only his teacher, Sybille, knew other than the Ravenkin and apparently the strange changeling child-woman, Kelly Rush ...or should he say, Aelish.

Now something else was calling him on the wind. He faltered for a moment, hearing an appalling tearing, ripping sound and a scream so loud, so close, the hairs on his arms stood on end.

A sense of bilocation, of otherworldliness, gripped him, accompanied by a sudden nausea and, despite the cold, he broke out in a clammy sweat. As suddenly as the sensation came, it was gone; leaving behind a feeling of such desolation he fell to his knees by the roadside - a need to curl into a foetal position overcame him and he wanted to cry like a child. She was gone, his teacher, his friend ...she was gone, only a small whisper left on the winds as the illusion of stillness passed and the rain fell again in relentless torrents.

In that moment he realised it wasn't just Sybille but Sam, who'd crashed through the veil with her. He heard music again... hauntingly sad, recognising it as the first song he'd created with Beth. Again, the laughter of the mad Dark Fae intermingled with the last sounds he'd heard before falling unconscious. Crystal shards sang; not just one but many...

'Dark colours spin a muted blight, each note a chorus of the night; spinning fast the dying light, upon the Skeins of Tyme.

We did not fall descent was slow, on gossamer wings in ebb and flow, we came, a planet's seeds to sow ...upon the Skeins of Tyme.

Then in sleep, we tumbled until the darkness every thread did fill. Humanity birthed, forsook her will …upon the Skeins of Tyme.

Webs are woven by intent, spiralling out the weave is bent. Earthly tides are almost spent …upon the Skeins of Tyme.

Grey the threads once coloured weave as all souls this realm must leave; that man himself could so deceive …the failing Skeins of Tyme.

Each mortal a thread that woven must, in perfect love and perfect trust; to rise above the cut and thrust …that snaps the Skeins of Tyme.

Where to mend and where to sew, loose threads fly no colours glow as all beyond this realm must go …into the Skeins of Tyme.

Through the gateway once, star bright, its edge now tainted by the blight, into shadow's darkest night…beyond the Skeins of Tyme.

Drifting through the warp and weft, fragile hands so pale and deft, weave the scrap of tapestry left …upon the Skeins of Tyme.

Flying spindle, curling thread, returning life the Earth to tread, once more Her Silvern blood is shed …upon the Skeins of Tyme.

Forgotten life, forsaken light, the silken threads are torn by blight, even the 'Onceborn' feel Her might …within the Skeins of Tyme.

Once Her threads so strong were tight, not to bind but to delight; to stretch, to hold our Souls winged flight ...into the Skeins of Tyme.

Willows bend and sway with ease; many kin feel her dis-ease, a chorus of sound, as mortal pleas ...pluck the Skeins of Tyme.

Who hears the call and follow must, with harm to none, fair and just, the clarion cry for love, for trust ...vibrates the Skeins of Tyme.

Each colour a note, a sound vibrating, within each sound, a memory, waiting, to reveal, new life awakening ...upon the Skeins of Tyme.

Sweet, discordant, flat or sharp, as the notes wrung from a harp; such songs lie, 'neath each beating heart ...upon the Skeins of Tyme.'

Along with the music, the smell of burnt feathers came to him on the gale. He pulled himself upright, gagging at the acrid odour and with a deep breath staggered on down the road to home. On reaching his crofters cottage he stumbled in through the door, always left unlocked, there being no need for locks and bolts out here in the Wildlands. He blinked as he saw the tainted webbing festooning everything and for a split second saw Honey lying dead on the hearth. Shaking his head he screamed, 'Your illusions are useless here; you can't get in without invitation, you soulless bitch! Do you think I don't know that?'

A warm wet muzzle snuffled at his hand and he greeted Honey, rubbing his hands over her thick coat and then feeding her as she galloped to the fridge to sit expectantly waiting. He then opened a small window, calling out in a low, guttural voice. In answer to his call, there came a loud 'caw' and a sleek Raven hopped in with another 'aaaark' of greeting and a flap of strong dark wings. Ruark, his other constant companion of late, looked at him, head on one side as she ruffled up her damp feathers sending a small shower of droplets over Morgan. 'Yeah thanks,' he said, 'as if I wasn't wet enough!' In his head, he heard clearly, in reply, *Youuuur late aaarrre!* 'What? Your my mother now?' he quipped and with a distinct, 'harrumph,' Ruark flew onto his shoulder.

Her huge beak would have daunted a lesser man and her claws, digging into his bare skin reminded him briefly of Kelly Rush's taloned fingers but without the malice. Morgan knew Ruark had an unusual restraint even for a Corvidae, especially with him. He'd found her caught in an unidentifiable and very sticky, black web of threads, hanging inverted in a huge old tree. She'd been very weak and he'd feared that the injuries to her wing and flight feathers would not heal well enough for her to ever fly again, but she'd proven him wrong and within an amazingly short space of time had regained her strength as he fed her what he could find.

Her wing bones straightened and her feathers regrew in a silvery colour like a streak of lightening, caught in the inky blue-blackness of her wing feathers ...or a line of stars in a dark, night sky.

He certainly hadn't expected her to stay, trying all possible methods to help her find her freedom again but she'd persisted in returning to him and was never more than a low call away from his cottage.

'Of course,' his relentless mind screamed at him and he heard again a peel of mirth. 'Ruark is Rowan, my Sam.' He sighed at the vision in hindsight, patting his pocket to feel the shape of her talisman bangle hidden there. He took it out, not wanting to expose it too long to this thread; he saw the markings change and move as if shifting a tempo of music up beat. Morgan placed it back in the pocket close to his heart, where he could hear it singing the same song of searching as the shards sang.

With a start he thought, 'If Ruark is here on this thread I need to keep her here. Sam and Ruark merged, but without the bangle Sam can't make the complete shift and without Sam, Ruark can't find their aspect Rowan. Rowan is sleeping within Ruark so the normal way of being has reversed itself.'

Looking around he felt a fondness for his little croft near Padarn in Cornwall and wondered if he would ever return there with Sam, the task almost overwhelming him..

His home was once ideal for his quite solitary life, but now he imagined extending it to create space for a studio for Sam... 'A family,' the laughter, which came again from the watching gathering, was hushed with a guttural word from The Morrigan. He brought his thoughts under control as he realised they were on view to his shifter-kin.

He could lose himself in his music and studies of the Druid Wytchways here, earning his money through making and repairing old musical instruments, playing when he could like tonight, with groups or soloists, needing someone to cover in an emergency or just because they'd heard of his musical prowess.

His life had been peaceful until tonight, when he'd heard the voice of his teacher calling to him by his Craft name and then the sense of her dissolving into the ethers, leaving only a fragile spark of her song behind.

A key to Sam's disappearance tied in with Aelish obviously but also with why the original death of her shaper body linked her with Sybille. He felt a tug on his consciousness as Ruark flew to the mantelpiece in the living room where she made her perch for the night, preening her ruffled feathers; her sharp claws had left scratchings like wild runes in the layers of ancient whitewash, baked to a glossy, hard sheen.

Loud in his ears he heard, 'Scratchings!' An excited little wren and a small, shiny pelted fox vixen sped away from the assembled group, nodding to the Lady as they did. He had the presence of mind to find pencil and tracing paper to take a rubbing of the markings on the mantle.

Then, for a while, he remembered nothing until he came too, with Sam bending over him. He made to sit up; embarrassed that she may have heard his thoughts, along with the hundreds of other shapers watching.

'Gently,' said Sam. 'Drink this Brandubh, it will quell the nausea.' Her gaze was intense as she scanned his body, mind and psyche. 'You need to rest now, we have much to do and I have a lot to tell you.'

'When you return, which you must,' she said quickly placing her hand on his heart where her bangle lay, before he could protest, 'no one must know where I am for the moment. I'll explain another time but the less you know the less you will have to speak to the others about. Now, you need to rest.'

Distracted he stared into the flames of a roaring fire, realising night had fallen and he'd been gone in his thoughts and memories for a whole day or more. Sam threw another log on and the dry tinder crackled, popping with a sudden greed as if a feeding frenzy had overtaken them; small wildfire salamander danced within. He felt the stirrings of a trance but brought himself back from the edge as he smelled the aromas of soup and bread and his gut rumbled in response to the natural call of hunger.

Knowing intuitively what Morgan needed, a small Fae-like creature brought him a bowl of steaming broth that smelt of the forest floor, together with fresh unleavened bread, crisp and sour from the nine woods of the need fire.

Relaxing a little, with the appeasement of his growling stomach, he thought long and deep of the woman who had taught him so much about himself, the ancient ways and of the Goddess who had chosen him as her own. She had always been there, teasingly, just on the peripheral of his vision and on the edge of his awakening ability to see Her there ...just waiting for him to remember. The Raven Goddess, 'The Morrigan'; not for the faint hearted. As yet, he'd not experienced Her wrath and hoped he never would.

He knew only that her love for Her convenors was fierce and undying. Once she claimed you there was no need to look anywhere else for anything else. Being an intense and somewhat solitary male, comfortable in his own company and that of his furred and feathered friends, his passion for music, his art and his thirst for continuing wisdom made him a daunting, albeit loyal friend. Now his thoughts had strayed to a new life, a relationship and family with Sam and then he slept, feeling the warmth of Sam's body close. He woke, cramped and confused on a couch in Robyn's living room, a crumpled sheet of paper, covered in bird-like scratchings, clutched in his hand.

Chapter 30
Loose Ends Meet Lost Pieces

I give myself to the Lord and Lady
…reaching within to find the flame.
Deep within the eternal silence
…only in the Lord and Lady's name.
None shall step across the border,
…between the lands of man and Fae.
None shall come to create disorder
…for lives shall fall in disarray

Flora woke from a dream where she'd been sitting listening to the dreams of another. She realised Vanessa had been there too, along with Pwyll, her mother, Jamie, Lily and Tara, who was fully restored to her shiny-feathered self. At that moment she realised Vanessa had been in fox form and it brought to mind Nessa's allusion to shape shifting the day before. 'Hmm, who were we watching dream' she hummed to herself, causing Cal to stir from deep within their huge old bed. They'd returned to Covenstead through the veil, leaving Vanessa to become accustomed to working the Northern Hemisphere energies.

'Morning love,' she whispered, letting the thought go for the moment.

'Morn'n,' Cal mumbled, rubbing his hands through rumpled hair. 'How did you both sleep?' He grinned sleepily, running his hands over Flora's little mounded belly; he felt a distinct pulse, like a ripple under water. He was instantly fully awake as they gazed at each other, in awe of the life growing and moving within her. Their child; their little shaper child.

Lily and Max had returned to their flat above Greenman Ways and were finally resolving all the difficulties Max had with her shaper gifts. Lily too had dreamed of the gathering; she'd been to many in her sleep but this one had seemed different. The Morrigan had been in attendance along with Branwen, Patron Goddess of small birds, who was also known as the White Crow. Was it Vanessa, she'd seen? She couldn't quite remember but the essence had been similar, if not the same.

Pwyll and Naboo had spent their night on the roof of the barn, listening to the gathering both on this thread and on the other; long disappeared into the Between. They couldn't remember, so deeply was it hidden away; as deeply as the Seer's Isle, they thought before spotting a rodent intruder to Flo's living space, they arrow dived together after it; not to kill but to warn the first autumn wanderer that this space was protected and off limits to their kind, especially at harvest time.

Beth had wandered back through the forests of the Between with Aithlin, unable to settle away from the wildwood bower, close to her little cottage in Wells.

When Max renovated the old stable barn he had discovered an old well covering, the cap gone but the old hand pump was still in working order after it was greased and oiled. She had always meant to explore the well, knowing it may be another route through the veil; in the dark she heard the sound of water dripping as the spring flowed and the song of the water sprites. She longed for the time, she hoped she'd eventually have, to bring her mother to the elders for healing.

Morgan's things were still around the place; his instruments and clothing lay on chairs, open books on the desk under the window. Study notes for his Druid training, which had become so much easier as he merged and linked with his aspect Bran to receive firsthand knowledge from the Bard and Cunningman.   She realised she'd missed his strong, masculine presence and felt her pang of loneliness, immediately soothed by a haunting sound of pipes. Morgan was back but she knew not completely, not yet and her Green Lord friend and lover, gone too. He had sacrificed himself for the burgeoning harvest time and now ran free and wild until Samhain called him home. This time of year was the most poignant, she missed his presence if only from a distance and as any human would, longed for the comfort of his arms around her as she pondered the tasks still to come and the rites still to enact.

She touched Mor's lute with gentle fingers and a rain of notes filled the room. She could hear the words of the song they had written and sung together; Skeins of Tyme and felt the air stir as new verses began to form, ready to 'download' as she called it.

She would sleep and see what came by morning; it came in her half sleep in a rush and she was excited to see if Mor had received it too.

Early the next morning she hurried through the veil, back to Robyn's farm. Concerned to see the blight edging the forest around, although it came no closer to the farm; Robyn's powers held it at bay but she wondered, not for the first time, if he was neglecting his duties as Spirit of Place in not working to keep the blight from anywhere else. He had professed he was only at half-strength with Sybille gone.

She found Morgan, bare foot and bare chested making a pot of coffee and preparing a huge pile of pancakes with wild berries for the crew she heard stirring around them. Vanessa emerged, tangle-headed, her face soft in sleepy lines. Robyn came in from outside, where he'd welcomed the sun of another day. Flo, Cal, Claire and Pwyll arrived through the veil, Susan and Alex from upstairs where they'd decided to spend the night, Lily and Max came by car from Glastonbury. Jamie, Maeve and Alma returned after a morning walk to the Tor. Rose had promised to attend as soon as she'd finished her work for the day and Lily was considering asking her to work at the shop. She had plenty of experience, was a first class Wytch and had previously told Lily she was looking for a couple of days work.

When everyone was there, they gathered in reverence for a new day and the fact that Morgan was back with them, though they doubted for long; he had an other-worldly look to him, much as Pwyll did when he returned from longer journeys through the Skeins. Over breakfast, they shared their dreams from the night before and Morgan was relieved they didn't remember much of what had transpired. None remembered Sam's presence as he felt her stir from sleep on the thread between threads where the Onceborn dwelt.

Then it was time to work. Morgan shared what pieces of his journey he could, leaving out The Morrigan's words and any allusion to Sam. Alma watched him carefully and he knew she was aware of Sam's location. Beth too had privately shared the journey she and Alma had made to find the Seer's Isle lost in the Myst and seeing him, Sam and Tara in the lands of the Firstborn. They spoke of the Tuatha de Danaan as the Shining Ones who left the world of man to move between the veils; only now, it would seem, they were emerging, as the Myth of the Celts described they would; when the world was in grave danger through negative Magicks.

Morgan told them about Kelly Rush and of Aelish's dark Magicks, cast over a Onceborn. He shared his thoughts for the safety of the real girl with the angel's voice and of the scratchings made in the plaster on the perch where Ruark roosted. He pulled the piece of folded paper from his shirt pocket, relieved it had made it through the veil, although he sensed The Morrigan had a hand in that.

Flo and Nessa brought out the Grimoire and the herbs, opening the book of shadows to a page they'd found that had the same strange, bird-like imprints over it. As if summoned, a host of tiny Fae in the bird forms flew in through the window, their sharp eyes focused on the markings. One by one, they each took a set of prints and followed them until it looked as if they danced a strange dance, flapping their wings. Every now and then they'd burst into discordant song. It wasn't like anything they'd heard before until Morgan, clamping his hands over his ears, yelped. 'That's it, the sound I heard when Sybille tore through the veil and Sam with her.'

'Yes,' Flo and Beth said as one. 'We heard it too on the day we received the letters from Sybille, although Sam was there with us so…? That does my head in,' Flo finished.

'Yeah,' Morgan replied, 'that weird sense of displacement when the threads collide.'

'It's similar to the markings that appeared on the floor in my studio after The Merrow,' 'Maeve tousled Alma's hair to take the sting out of her words. 'They looked like bird footprints.'

'Well then,' said Cal in his practical manner, 'let's see what we can put together for Mabon and Ostara, shall we?'

Together with Sam, Flora and Vanessa, Cal had researched more of the herbs from Airmhid's bag through smell and texture, some still recognisable by their colouring, although again they were loath to taste them for fear of poisoning. Cal, however, had the idea to send them to a friend of his that worked in the forensics section at the Uni in York where Cal had been working and there were some rare finds indeed amongst the samples he'd sent for analysis; original strains of ancient seeds, pods and berries, root, leaf and flower. The most astonishing discovery was that they still held a life force so high, they could have been picked and dried only weeks ago; in fact that life force seemed to increase every time Flora opened a packet to research it.

Samantha had been recording it all and helping with the research, her interest, piqued by the history they revealed, had led her to ask Flora's permission to start a Grimoire of the findings and their medicinal and magickal properties, to which she'd agreed with excitement. Therefore, it was they drew together: researcher, historian, anthropologist, archaeologist, herbalist; all Wytches. Morgan too, putting in ideas and information as he remembered snippets from his studies with Sybille on Magickal Herb craft.

Each picked up a snatch of tune as the packets, the Grimoire and the sheets of parchment in the Book of Shadows hummed their strange, cacophonic songs. One by one, the birds would approach, dancing on a particular piece of text until the sounds became a little quieter, gentler and then Beth and Morgan would try to make it something they could work with for an invocation. They began to see that the birds avoided some and focused on others. When anyone went near a different text the birds would scold them, intervening to keep them away until they could all clearly see the herbs to use and the beginnings of a chant had formed.

They found the herbs they needed, carefully measuring and blending, chanting together to enhance the strength but also to make Sam aware, wherever she was, they were coming to find her soon.

They planned the rites for both hemispheres and when all was done they became as warriors training at Scathach's Hearth. They knew Mabon and Ostara were probably a trial run, but no less important to get right. After that it was only eight weeks to Samhain and Beltane and then the thread would run its course. They studied, meditated and dreamed together; each time their journeywork took them deeper and deeper into the Skeins of Tyme.

Chapter 31
Weaving a Web

The guiding reign of pure intent, forgotten in the deep,
…is now ascending …pulling, to awaken us from sleep.
The web of light around this orb,
…our home away from home,
…birthed simply for Her Light to feel,
…the darkness of alone.

Just as before, Vanessa sang as she prepared the circle for the rite. In part, it would be a repetition of last year's Ostara Rite but this time, each would hang their eggs on the tree in silence and each egg held the same plea that Sybille and Sam come home to them. There was nothing anyone wanted other than that; they felt very empty of need.

Robyn and Rose, who greeted Vanessa with fondness as the daughter of her one time friend, had decorated the circle in brightly coloured spring flowers, hyacinth, blue bell, harebell, freesia, jonquils, crocus and flowering plum and cherry blossom. It looked festive but none of the seven working the Northern Hemisphere rite felt like celebrating, despite the fact that the honouring of the turning wheel was still the major reason Wytches worked the seasonal rites.

Rose was a beautiful woman, one who grew lovelier as she aged, 'Just as Sybille did,' Vanessa thought, thinking of the gentle woman who had trained her own mother in the Old Ways. Living close to Glastonbury, she mentioned her daughter Nyla who, born in Australia, Rose was trying to convince to come live in the UK. To date, this hadn't happened but she was hopeful it would. Vanessa promised to look her up in Melbourne when she could.

Lily was strong in her circle casting and working, Max becoming more adept. With the addition of Aerandir, who would stand beyond the circle's edge, Jamie, Maeve and Robyn old hands, Vanessa was feeling a little more confident and sang as she swept the circle space in preparation. She could feel the surges of spring energy flowing up her legs through the soles of her feet. It traversed her spine, leaving a warm tingle where it coursed, which settled in her womb, a small flame in a cauldron. She sang again of renewal, of new beginnings, new projects in fact, new life or in this instance retuning life…

'*Three times the circle round …thrice to bless this sacred ground. As the flowers bloom and small birds sing …to welcome in the spring,*' …the birds fell silent in the trees, causing her to pause in alarm. 'What's the matter?' she called out. 'I didn't think my voice was that bad,' and to her horror saw fragrant blossoms wilting, turning black and decayed,

Silence; she saw Aerandir struggling with keeping the edge of the circle clear of the encroaching blight and froze in her tracks. There was no sign of the others who would be preparing themselves indoors as dark threads of sticky web began to cascade down over the circle.

Thinking fast, all the tools cleansed and waiting on the altar, the herbs and oils were prepared, ready for the Rite, she began the fastest circle casting ever performed and alone; she was alone as the yellow, stinking fog descended, hearing even the cries of her friends struggling to reach her diminish, until there was only her and the silence.

She cast with a bright Athame, her mother's she realised; where it had come from, she had no idea.

Consecrating the water, '*I exorcise thee oh creature of water of all impurities and uncleanliness from the spirit of the world of phantasm, wherefore do I bless and consecrate thee.*'

'*Blessings be upon this creature of salt, let all malignancies and hindrances be cast forth hence from and all good enter herein, wherefore do I bless thee.*'

She worked quickly and accurately, stirring the salt and water three times round to blend and bless; she couldn't afford to think her casting would not be enough to keep out the dark but her breath hitched as she walked the circle.

'*Earth and Water where thou art cast, let no evil purpose last, in complete accord with me. As I do will so mote it be.'* As she splashed the blessed earth and water elements, the ground hissed where it fell and the dark retreated.

She lit the self-igniting incense with shaking hands and walked again the circle round, building the walls of smoke as wet, slapping noises hit the ground around.

Following through, her heart missing beats, until she heard a voice in her head saying *'Breathe, little one, breathe.'* 'Aerandir,' she almost sobbed his name as she lit the quarter candles, managing to seal the circle with fire.

Once more grasping the Athame in shaking, sweat slicked hands, she moved to the centre of her circle…

'I cast thee oh circle that thou be the boundaries between the realms of men and the realms of the mighty ones. A guard and protection, which will preserve and contain the energies I do raise within thee, therefore do I bless and consecrate thee.'

All thought of the traditional words of welcome and greeting to the spring were gone, immaterial in a cold, foul smelling world.

She sank to her knees. So much depended on her as she struggled to remember the Rite they had so carefully constructed.

Breathing hard, she wiped her hands on her robe, before removing it to stand, willow-slender and tall, sky clad. Even the noise of the wet threads, hitting her circle confine, dimmed into silence as she stood, defiantly; pulling herself upright.

Standing at each quarter and cross quarter, she called the elements and the Lord and Lady to watch over her and bless her rite of offering. For a brief moment, the fog parted and she clearly saw her mother, standing tall, facing down a violently snarling Dark Fae with Aerandir for support. Of her friends, Rob and Rose, there was no sign.

Gathering herself, she approached the Altar again, reaching for the herbs to blend for the ritual. It struck her that what they'd planned was not what presented itself now; she would have to improvise. She searched her mind for the hidden knowledge, calling out to Nina to help her make the right choices.

'Agrimony, I call your name, fragrant Belladonna and fiery Wolf's Bane …' she faltered, praying the herbs were in the bag.

'Angelica, protect me from a creature gone insane …Mandrake, help me clear the circle …Periwinkle, cleanse my psyche again.'

She had no idea where the words came from or the knowledge of the herbs but they were all there waiting in little dishes on the Altar.

Opening her arms as if to pull down the sun she sang, her sharp, clear notes breaking through the veil.

'Lord and Lady of dark and light, cleanse my soul of this false veiled night, Guard and protect, through the mist-torn veil. May her attacks be foiled …let goodness prevail.

Spring has come and the birds fly free …I feel the surge; sap rises in me. May the gods be kind and in friendship bring …the return of mentor, and sister kin.'

Meanwhile the others, unaware of the drama unfolding outside, mixed the blends for cleansing, showered and robed; they believed Vanessa and Rob were setting up the ritual space. The cold dawn air held a static hiss of stormy energy perfect for the working. Each knew their role: unspoken, unwritten; each would bring all of themselves to the working, but suddenly as the last preparations were made, they walked outside and into a blanket of fog reeking of sulphur.

'SHIT!' Max yelled, 'Vanessa's alone out there. Rose, where's Rob?' He looked to the elder with deference.

'Jamie, what do we do?' said Maeve.

Aerandir and Rob appeared out of the fog. 'It's okay, she's coping magnificently,' Robyn almost crowed with delight.

'You can be this pleased, when young Vanessa is facing off Goddess knows what?' Lily threw at him.

Reaching out Rose soothed her. 'They know what they're doing Jay-Lily. You have to trust.'

'Truly. It's okay. She's built a circle nothing can penetrate, which gives us time to defend her when she closes the circle down. Aelish won't be able to hold this for much longer,' Rob indicated the fog around them. 'She'll be exhausted soon though,' he thought.

'You mean we have to wait this out?' Max said in agitation. 'Are you sure she's safe?'

'I'm sure lad, I'm sure.'

From within the fog they could hear faint chanting and as they walked quietly around the circle edge, Robyn instructed them to pull their hoods up and as far down over their faces as possible; he splashed them liberally with a protective essence blended from Juniper, Sage and Nettle. As they walked, they could hear slapping sounds when the thick strands of blighted web, whipped against the cone of power of Vanessa's circle. They couldn't see what she was doing within but the energy was holding and her chant lingered in the air. Every now and then, they would see a flash of light as her spell worked its Magick against the encroaching dark. Blighted strands lashed at them but the essence worked and the webs dropped, withering to the ground.

Aerandir worked his way around to the South East, edging toward the perimeter of the sturdy circle energy. He hoped his timing was right as he drew an Elder wand with a black onyx tip cut like an arrowhead. He carefully, ceremoniously, cut a doorway into the circle as Vanessa finished her invocation. Jamie watched his back, an iron blade drawn that caused Aerandir to flinch and even Rob kept a wide birth.

Aerandir stepped through into the aqua blue smoke of Vanessa's energy. She lay on the ground naked, her skin white and as he watched, threads of blight writhed across her chest and belly, falling to the earth, consumed by her bright aura mixed with clean, loamy soil.

He quickly threw his cloak over her as she stirred, opening eyes bright with unshed tears. She looked as if she was recovering from a fever, he thought. Thanking the Bright Lady that Nessa was okay, he carried her out of the circle. Rob's essence had cleared the space around and the sun was beginning to filter through the trees as a spring morning dawned.

Maeve and Lily moved carefully into the circle - chanting, building power…

*'In circle bright …in circle round …we spin the threads on sacred ground. Where life begins and all life ends …we summon those whose energy lends …to cleansing here in timeless space …releasing Vanessa from this place …to what we will …that we may see …*THIS WE DO WILL …SO MOTE IT BE!'

Without a word to the others, Aerandir carried Vanessa away, through the forest and through the veil to the little cottage in the forest. She made no sound, only looked at him wide eyed as he drew a warm, scented bath for her and when she hadn't the strength to climb in, he removed his cloak from around her and gently lowered her in, keeping his eyes fixed on hers. She felt no embarrassment only thankfulness that it was he and that she was safe.

In a rush of air and a rustle of wings, Claire and Flora manifested. Changing mid-flight, they took in the scene at a glance.

'It would seem we're not needed,' said Claire, smiling at the faint flush on Aerandir's cheeks.

'Come on Aerandir; show me how you make that beautiful woody tasting tea, would you? I never get it quite right.' Flora led him from the bathroom.

Claire washed Vanessa's hair, still filled with particles of black web, calling out to Flo when Vanessa slipped into shock. They administered rescue remedy and a light potion to relax her shivering, rigid body and then tucked her into the huge canopied bed. Aerandir slipped quietly in to sit by her side. Nina's voices calmed him. 'She just needs to rest Fae-kin; she'll be fine by morning.' Aerandir pulled an old overstuffed chair next to the bed, curling his long frame into it, while he watched the night through.

Claire and Pwyll came and went; the entire Ravenkin passed through with Morgan as he left again for the world between.

Back at Rob's farm, slowly the residue of fog and ichor disappeared, consumed by their circle cleansing. Then, instead of the cold and gloomy start to the day, suddenly the sun burst through the clouds and the frost began to melt. Water ran in small rills that sped down the hill and dripped off rooftops into water tanks.

A ring of burnt ground remained after they'd cleansed and cleared everything within and without. Annie's Athame was missing and weeks later, when Vanessa searched, it was back in her mother's box with all the other tools.

Chapter 32
Darkest Places

Follow the pathway of your dreams.
Create the scenarios in your mind.
What thoughts inhibit your success?
What happens in the process to make you blind
...to the fact that success is yours within
...in your head, your heart ...it's under your skin.
Be aware ...dare to dream as the calling is heard
...take a chance ...spreads your wings and take flight
...be as free as a bird

As Vanessa slept she travelled to the Birthing Tree where deep within Nature's Heart, in Her rich, moist, fertile cradle, something awoke. Not in a slow, stirring, stretching, awakening but in a 'snap to' moment.

The Spirit of the Forest of Secrets, known to most as Herne the Hunter, heard the call and turned the focus inwards to the place of greening, burgeoning life. The tiny seed, offshoot of the Birthing Tree, was sending down its own first tentative roots that reverberated through all the realms on the Skeins of Tyme.

Down it went, through the plant and mineral kingdoms, to the earth elemental realm and deeper still, into the molten heart of Terra. Reflecting off an enormous, multifaceted crystal shard, a remnant of the original planetary core, it sent out a pure signal, a sound so sweet, for an instant for only an instant, it was felt by the Onceborn and Firstborn alike as a time to hold the breath and listen, enchanted. In Maeve's bag, the shards of crystal rang out, vibrating in sweet sad tones, calling to the Mother lode.

Further, out it went through the Elven, the Fae races realms of light. Out to the centre of creation where the Makers, gleaming like crystalline stars, pulsed even brighter in their tending of the Trueshapers stirring in their gossamer cocoons. Ever spreading, like a net of fine silken threads, each thread a colour, a note, sounding in joy and triumph announcing the imminent birth of a new awakened one.

In that same instant the radar screens and tracking systems of every government security in all of Terra stopped. Strange signs appeared on the screen for a moment like tiny, bird print scratchings. Then a small, shining, split-winged being of pearlescent light was briefly, seen, accompanied by one clear note, heard throughout all the realms before it fell, corrupted, withered and blackened as it felt the fear, the war and the carnage that had been created by humans on the planet. In a brief moment of life, its light winked out and was gone.

The Trueshapers renewing themselves stirred as they felt the fall, a ripple of terror like a sullen wave swept through their realm. At the same moment, stillness, darkness came for the first time in the realms of light. As one seedling of the Birthing tree died, one small Maker fell, catapulting into the cocoon where the Trueshaper Silver and her renewing Littleshape, Sybille, slumbered. Torn from the cocoon, the Trueshaper flew to the Birthing Tree. She called the Makers to assist in creating another cocoon, while cradling the comatose Littleshape, attempting to bring back her spark of life from the void, where it had fallen with the tainted Maker.

Flora stirred in her sleep as the tiny foetus felt the heartbeat of its birth mother and its planetary Mother combined. She felt a moment of blind panic for the unborn shifter in her belly.

'It will be alright,' the tiny embryo whispered to her and to Sybille and Sam as they fell through the veil. This time Sam was ready, taking the falling Littleshape to the places Between where she walked with the Firstborn.

Chapter 33
Sybille's Song

Where will I be when this life sets me free? ...when this body is frail and bent Will there be signs that shall guide me? Who will be there at the top of the stair, to wipe away tears and stroke my white hair? Will I find my way through intent?
Musings from the personal journal of Sybille Madison

After Sam had visited the Birthing Tree, catching Sybille as she fell, Vanessa had become agitated; it felt as she imagined it would feel if she were pregnant as she felt the frantic stirrings in her belly as Sybille's essence became more conscious.

In her sleep, she had a visit from Silver and it was a rare occurrence for a Trueshaper to make contact with anyone, even their own Littleshapes, unless they had progressed enough to understand the implications.

She sat reading Sybille's work on the passage of the three souls of humankin, first not understood, as this in itself was the journey of the Way of the Wise, the experiential way of the Wytch.

The first layer, she read, was what governed the physical manifestation, the body that housed the mental self, humankin called ego. In truth, this was a composite, in itself, of many Littleshape memories, gathered into one coherent moment on the time continuum. Tiny fragments of memory, written in the cells of a frail, yet so resilient, human frame. Any memory of where it had been and what it was now, watered down by the inability to maintain awareness as it descended deeper and deeper into the earth realm's torpid energy.

In its constant search for truth, it had fallen into the illusion of time as a straight line, from past to present and into a perceived future. This stretched the Skeins of Tyme so thinly, just one thread only remained, attaching each human life to the web. Pausing, she asked Aerandir, her constant companion, how this would have affected Sybille if the fine umbilical thread tore itself away from the Mother.

'It would be difficult to remember who you were,' he replied. 'Without at least that attachment, even the Firstborn fall into forgetfulness.'

Thoughtfully she continued reading…

The second, Higher or Soul self as the humankin called it, the Trueshaper, was the one who gathered the threads of life experience needed to weave the relevant memories into a tapestry, for the journey back to full awareness of Oversoul, of Goddess self, the third component in the layered soul's essence.

She tried to understand the stark reality that things could go wrong even in the higher realms of life, if Sybille, separated from her Trueshape whilst journeying to renew, could cause the web of life to break.

Every time Sybille had disappeared on her previous sabbaticals, it was a conscious journey and so she must be a person of extraordinary awareness, very near to becoming a Trueshaper.

Silver whispered in her head. 'You have understanding of the information given that most humankin would baulk at but here you are as stalwart as you have always been and it is for this reason that you hold the hope of Sybille's recovery, together with Rowan's, in your hands. There will be help, as much as we can give you, but the work in the physical realms must be your task and each of your sisterkin has had or will have a role to play and now, this time it is yours.

Your Fox-shifter blood makes you very different to your friends, but it's those variances that temper the more Fae indifference to human feelings and the human feelings that can totally overwhelm you.'

She stretched, feeling recovered and more relaxed after her Ostara ordeal, ready to face the group and to hear how the Mabon Rite had progressed.

Aerandir walked her back through the forest to Rob's where everyone was meeting. Seeing the circle of burnt ground, she hesitated but his firm hand on her back steadied her as he led her into the house.

Chapter 34
Mabon's Light

A ghost of autumn lingers on
...the scratching of leaves
...a whispered bird song
...but she waits in the night
...breathe her scent, feel her might,
...in the lightning storm
...at the cold edge of dawn,
...in the rumbling thunder
...hold your breath don't go under;
...for fear's not the way
...it will flee before day
Winter ice clears the way
...to where the frost giants play.

Everyone was horrified at what had happened to Vanessa at the Ostara Rite, but thankfully the Mabon ritual had passed uneventfully; in fact, they felt a little let down.

They had cast the circle and enacted the Autumn Rite as they had in the previous season, with the addition of an invocation to bring their friends home. Just as before, there was no response.

Morgan had stayed to participate; restless, he left soon after to return to find Sam but before he left, he and Beth had brought the final verses of their song together.

They realised it told their story and were heartened to think that the positive ending described in the lyrics would come about in reality.

Claire, Pwyll, Cal, Flora, Morgan, Alex and Susan, with Aithlin on the outer rim, cast the circle flawlessly.

They celebrated the age-old story of autumn harvest with apple bobbing and other such traditions

Equinox brought balance to the world but for them it wasn't the usual, happy, friendly gathering as the blight stalked the perimeter of the circle but most of the attention from Aelish, focused on Vanessa in Glastonbury, catching her vulnerable and alone.

It wouldn't happen again they all vowed and at no time did any of them even walk in the garden alone.

They finished gathering in the Harvest fruits, grapes and the last blackberries ripe on vines and bramble hedgerow. Elderberries hung in fragrant umbels, juicy and sticky with dew so the following morning they planned to pick and bottle, make elderberry wine, liquor and cough tinctures. No matter what, they were determined to make life at Covenstead as normal as possible for as long as they could.

Flora, now in the third month of the first trimester, was happy to watch the others climb ladders and cart baskets of soft fruit. They'd left this last batch specifically to ripen well for the natural sugar content to rise, the better for the liquid produce they would create, what remained would be used for dye making ruby dyes and inks.

Another season passed and the entire group, grubby and tired, stopped for the day to sit in the afternoon, autumn sunlight but not for long as the chill came on stealthy feet to frost the grass with ice. Taking their glasses and food inside, they settled round Sybille's old and beautiful table to finish their meal.

Morgan surprised them by dropping by again to say hello, reassure them that Sam was better than expected but wouldn't elaborate and to send Sam's love to them all. Things were on the move and he suggested they prepare for more attempts by Aelish to hinder them at every possible opportunity. He was shocked to hear of her blatant attack on Vanessa and thanked Aerandir for his care of her.

'Everyone rallied round,' Aerandir said in a matter of fact manner but Morgan had already noted his eyes barely left Vanessa and that he sat opposite her, the better to watch her every move.

'Love blooms at strange times,' he thought to himself as he looked around the room of familiar and dear faces. He hoped soon that he and Sam might share the same joy as he saw on Cal and Flora's faces or Lily's and Max.

He gathered with the others to sing with Beth and Vanessa and to his surprise, Aerandir joined them, singing in a pure alto; of Aithlin there was no sign.

In the whispering leaves is a song …in the sound of the wind a chord. In the notes of each chorus of birds …is a fountain of echoing words.

Hold tight to a dream of healing …and to all that you will for your friends. When you sing the notes together …there's a story that never ends.

Each refrain you hear in the sunlight …on the winds or through a dark night …if you listen, you'll hear her calling …her words will dispel the blight.

In tones of hidden meaning, her words will be only for you …words, when with love strung together …will glow in a many-coloured hue.'

Chapter 35
Alma Remembers

Her heart is silent ...her wings are frail
...she heals other's suffering and in turn will ail
...but she will find the way to the edge of time
...hearing the night calls, following the rhyme
...and the rhythm of life as it ebbs and flows
...to the circle of stones where the Magick knows
...all the answers, hidden deep in her soul.
She will find her way to the edge of time
...where the Crooked Path leads her to her goal.

Time meant nothing in the realms Between and to the little water Merrow once known as Alma, it was only a memory. On this thread, she was fully conscious and she sat remembering how the last ritual had played itself out and what her part was in the whole.

She remembered before she had woken up again, remembering her tasks that, occasionally, she received flashes of herself as a human child held in soft but strong, feminine arms and knew that in her once human aspect she must have had a mother, parents perhaps. She hugged the thought to her that Maeve and Jamie would be looking for her; they'd have her back always although they didn't realise she was no child and had never been. Now she had a choice to make as the weave unravelled and with it so must she.

When she'd been asleep to all the good things she'd discovered, it hadn't taken much to distract her. There was so much fun to have in seeking out little gifts to give M'lady or to secrete away in little nooks and crannies to gloat over later. She was like a magpie, constantly collecting things that had no apparent value to their owners. They wouldn't leave them lying around if they did.

Pain hurt her physically she remembered and that had been the reason she'd manifested with a physical body, to experience it but it was always the most well received gift from M'lady.

Alma would occasionally take everything out to look at and try on, pinning a broach here or a feather there with equal pleasure. She tried several times to wear the beautiful snood Maeve made Bethan for her naming day, but it was uncomfortable and left her feeling irritated. One day it snagged in her hair, tearing her scalp as she fought to remove it; a terrible feeling of despair came over for a moment but she couldn't recognise the source. It sounded as though someone was wailing in grief and loss, but then she realised the sound came from her and she flung the hurt filled thing away as far as she could, giving in to the very human depths of sorrow. Again an experience she'd come to have firsthand on the physical threads in the Skeins.

She'd almost given the snood to Aelish and she'd not understood why the beautiful thing had held so much pain and why the stones felt familiar. Then she recalled giving some glassy shards to M'lady, having found them lying unwanted under a table, in the elder Stregga's room, where she lay unconscious. Fear had overcome her and she'd curled whimpering in the corner of her little hideaway; strange visions playing out in her head of a red haired human woman; what was her name; a smiling Foxkin and a dark haired Cunningman of Magicks.

'Look to the darkness in broken change…' she whispered to herself. **'Broken change,'** she yelled aloud, bringing herself from her reverie. Echoing through the Between it was heard by the earth and water sprites.

She'd again been distracted by a glittery thing and picking up a finely wrought bracelet of silver, polished it against her sleeve until it sang and shone with light. Unearthly sounds rang out through the Aether …sounds of such beauty and richness, Sam stirred in her sleep in the thread of the Firstborn, tears leaking from eyes, dry from remembered flaming heat, longing flooded her for something lost long ago.

In that moment, Alma knew exactly what she had to do. Picking up the bracelet from where it lay, she returned through the veil to the well Max had discovered when he renovated the stables. From there she slipped again through the veil to Bethan, appearing on the day of the Lammas rite when Sam had vanished. Breathlessly she instructed Beth to give the bracelet to Morgan rather than directly to Sam, when the moment came this time should Sam return for the final Samhain Rite.

'What do you know Alma?' Beth asked her. Looking into the emerald pools of Alma's eyes, she knew. 'Alma, there has to be another way. Maeve can't lose you again.'

'Oh I'll see you again Lady. I always come again.'

Chapter 36
Last Chance

My body ...a vessel, created to hold my song
...for right or wrong
...we cannot judge its meaning
If we try ...perhaps tomorrow, die
...within each note, there are my truths still gleaming.

Days turned into weeks, with Morgan coming and going between threads. He was training with the Firstborn and each appearance showed him stronger, fitter and more relaxed. Jamie was training Cal, Max and Alex in strength and endurance and Maeve was teaching Vanessa, Susan and Lily with Claire giving a hand. As a shifter, she had a natural edge on strength and endurance. Flo would watch and all had vowed to protect her, as she was unable to take the gruelling training Maeve meted out, contenting herself with a gentle stretch programme. Happy to potter, her pregnancy advanced and she took on a glow of such beauty, people would blink, just looking at her.

Every now and again, she'd call into Earthly Rites to check on the state of business but it all seemed in hand, especially with Rose coming and going through the veil to do most of the management for them. She did, however warn them that people were beginning to get a little suspicious of their disappearing for days, even weeks on end and were still asking after Sybille constantly.

After numerous meets, Rob had finally told them about his times with both The Cybil and Sybille. He refused to say any more about Alma for some reason, although Beth had a different perspective, merely saying she thought Alma would tell her story soon enough. Maeve and even Jamie didn't quite understand what there was to tell but Alma always managed to disappear whenever she came up in discussion.

Now they gathered to discuss and make final plans for the crucial Samhain Rite.

They had each written a piece they would say, a statement of who they were and the gifts they brought in service …the herbs selection had been the hardest thing but they became more confident in their choices as the day drew closer.

In sudden inspiration, Beth had remembered the beautiful cloak her grandmother Circaea had gifted her, which had been her mother's ceremonial robe.

'What will we do with it Beth?' Vanessa queried. 'Surely you can't mean to use it for Samhain?'

'No Nessa, this is for Beltane, I'm not sure why but I think instead of splitting in two groups as before it should just be you, Flo, Maeve and I.'

'I'm not sure how the other's will take it after what happened at Ostara though.'

'Well they'll just have to trust my judgement on this one, won't they?' she said with an enigmatic smile and a flicker of change to her Arianwen aspect.

'Fine then,' she grinned, 'I for one won't argue with her.'

Vanessa finding the book of shadows and the wand was something that could change their whole approach to the Samhain ritual. Cal and she had begun to confer a little, out of earshot of everyone. They both held key knowledge yet couldn't risk going against the wishes of Hercurin and so they shared between each other the thoughts of how it should be featured into the ritual without drawing Aelish's attention prematurely. Beth was intuitive enough to understand what was going on and asked Alma to bring the snood from where she'd hidden it.

Before they knew it, there was only a week left and they were filled with a sense of dread. None felt ready but Tara, returning fully recovered from her ordeal, told them to trust and that there were many who would arrive to assist them, even if unseen.

Exhausted, they sat outside at Wells; it was a cold clear afternoon and their murmuring voices, interspersed with snatches of song, carried through the trees surrounding Beth's home.

Morgan and Alma stood next to the old well which didn't appear to feature on any map of the area and which seemed occasionally to shift position slightly. It had a glow around it at this time of afternoon as the sun sank in the West behind it. Alma whispered to Morgan but clammed up when anyone else approached.

Maeve was beginning to get a little irritated by the continued undercurrent of secrecy that now enveloped Alma. Something was changing and she couldn't work out what.

With nothing planned about Beltane, Beth took the moment to explain what she wanted to do in Glastonbury, but not why. Maeve was astounded when no one quizzed her. Only Aerandir, seeing the glamour that Beth put about her like a cloak, smiled a knowing smile, saying nothing.

With time to be for a while the friends planned and schemed, each adding something new they'd observed over the past weeks and slowly the Samhain Rite took on a life of its own.

On Samhain Eve in Wells they sat in silence; a band of warriors facing the war ahead. No one knew what the outcome would be victory or defeat.

Chapter 37
Dreaming of Renewal at Beltane

In the night with Wytchlight shining
...none shall pass across the veil.
Cup and blade now realigning
...sending sparks across the trail.
One shall come, pale and fragile
...to renew the Skeins of Tyme.
Innocent and without guile
...a will of iron to break frost's rime

Dawn at Beltane, in the forest near Rob's farm, the girls gathered alone. They wished Sam could be there but were confident that after the Samhain working she would re-join them and so Flora, Maeve, Vanessa and Bethan cast the working circle and Minhiriath's cloak came to life. Spirits of air lifted it; swirling out and across the floor like a wash of water as the spirits entered.

Buds and greening leaves burst with the spirit of earth and rainbow colours reflected as the crystal pieces sparked fire, crystals from the origins of the planet's volcanic power embedded in the wand Cal had made and the delicate snood of Maeve's creating, fashioned with tiny shards from the original splintered piece.

They chanted as Maeve, Flora and Vanessa lifted the cloak, spreading it around Arianwen's shoulders; the snood held her heavy hair, appearing to incorporate itself into the hood, the wand held across her breast like a small spear.

They began to chant the now familiar rhymes Sybille had given them; Vanessa sang Sam's part…

'Earth you are, from earth you came, your intellect from Air you gain. Your Fire should burn, with flaming ire; Yet Water has put out your fire.

Fire is harsh and anger sings; don't go too close you'll burn your wings. Earth yourself go deep within; let Water again become your kin. Let Air breath you, let laughter ring.

Earth you are, compassion grown, Fire and Water, becoming known. Air will sing, when Fire alights and Water washes all things bright.

Spirit sings within your frame, on your loom and through your pain. Water washes all things clean; Air brings truth to you again. Fire needed, Earth to ground, when the web you weave, all things abound.'

Adding the fifth verse created for the rite…

'Spirit the thread that binds the four, creating the pathway through the door, to the light that streams across verdant ground and the crystals sing their sacred sound. As the fifth combines, the wheel turns on and the fire of the Mother, heard in the song.'

As the cloak fell around her in glimmering folds, in a flash of light Bethan saw a host coming toward her, changing as they did; known and unknown faces, so many other aspects, merging and morphing. Her own face changed constantly to match, from young to old and back again.

All the emotions of every human life and every human quality passed across her face …anger, fear, resentment and pain, as much as joy and wisdom. As she moved closer, Beth could see The Cybil, Leah and all the other missing aspects but instead of heading for Silver where she stood on the edge of their circle, they moved toward her. She saw no sign of Sybille.

'No,' she thought, 'this can't be, they must all return to their Trueshape,' but as she watched, Silver too, her wounds healing, drifted toward her. The Fae stood in a circle and a flickering shape that looked like Hercurin appeared on the rim; all the small creatures that inhabit the Beyond clustered around him. She knew it must be a sending; Hercurin couldn't leave his home ground and where he dwelled it was Samhain.

She could step back as Bethan if she would, to a mortal life or she could step forward and embrace the wholeness of Arianwen, her Green-cloaked self. She could be with Hercurin, merge and blend to become the spirit of place for all the wells and springs, rivulets and ponds of the planet, Lady Arianwen once more.

Beth saw the faces of her friends around the edge and hesitated before she changed; her Arianwen aspect emerged again, horns raised; neck long and proud. They watched, briefly glimpsing The Cybil, Leah and so many other soul-aspects, converged, merging with Arianwen.

Bethan flinched just for a second before the watching group saw their friend smile blissfully, stepping into her Trueshape's embrace. A note and then another sounded, Makers swarmed and sprites danced as Arianrhod stepped from the Between to join Arianwen and merging ...became one in Spirit.

Watching in awe the women moved in a circle around Bethan where she lay, enveloped in her mother's translucent cloak of iridescent colours. Bethan, their friend, clever weaver and musician looked unchanged except for the glow of wisdom that emanated from every pore of her skin.

She woke, sitting up and stretching as if she'd simply had a good night's sleep. Smiling at the concerned faces she said, 'Okay crew, let's get back to Wells and kick arse!'

Maeve laughed '...I'm confused, shouldn't you be all otherworldly and mysterious all the time now?'

Bethan broke into peels of rippling laughter, 'Well hmm, let's see,' and she shifted in an instant from Bethan to the embodiment of her Goddess Trueshape and back again.'

'Point taken!'

'Come on then, let's go do what the Lady commands,' said Flo.

'Hold hands,' Beth reached out with hers to Vanessa and Flo; transporting them through the aethers to the waiting group in Wells.

Chapter 38
Aelish and Rowan

In each cell of your being ...a memory lies
...it's not found in the aethers ...nor in deep blue skies
...when you remember ...when you awake
...who are you truly ...what form, will you take?

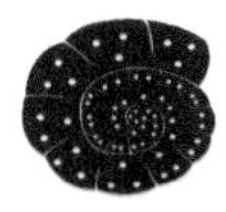 Rowan was a Firstborn, a Ravenshaper of The Morrigan's brood. She was fearless and yet had compassion for all living things. Years ago, in human time span, she'd watched the wheel turn, observing the entanglements of Fae and humankin and aware of the Dark Fae Aelish Farandirim's passion for the Druid Brandubh.

Rowan was aware of the young Druid but knew it would be a mistake for a Shaper to become emotionally involved with a human, whose life was set as a Cunning-man, a healer for his tribe and for any who needed his wisdom; he had the makings of a Merlyn. She could not stop what her heart felt, only try to ignore its increased rhythm whenever she set eyes on the tall, burnished haired man and yet it wasn't him she saw when she looked at him; it was another, swarthier, with Raven dark hair and eyes as blue as the Morrigan's Firstborn.

They often saw each other but had never really spoken, both knowing their attraction was not something they would follow through to an outcome. 'Another thread,' she would whisper, 'another time in your human reckoning,' hoping he would hear and understand.

He did, Brandubh was after all a Cunningman. He had premonitions of other threads where their lives had been intertwined and wished he could remember every detail that he might ease the soreness he felt as a physical thing in his chest whenever he saw the dark haired Ravenshaper. He was also aware of the other, a Dark Fae who stalked him at every turn, one moment sultry with fiery passion in her eyes, then quicksilver-fierce when she saw where his feelings lay.

Aelish Farandirim would not let a Shaper come between her and her prey. Aelish had moved between threads through the worlds between worlds, always coming back to the moment when she had first seen Bran. She had stalked him through lives, always wanting until she had seen the way of revenge as the only option for what ailed her, for he did not care. There had been a fleeting moment when her glamour had almost drawn him in but his Magicks were far too strong for him not to recognise the machinations of her kind.

Everything she had ever done, based on this; kill shapers, harm those who had anything to do with the soul she wanted above all others. It was why she brought about the destruction of Pwyll's happiness, because of his connections to Bran through the Shaperkin. Through this she missed the thread bringing that very soul to her, this time through her own body - her son Morgan, who could never be hers in the way she craved.

Rowan, a seer to match Morgan's powers, was aware of all the potential that could occur but was powerless to act. Only the Lady and the Fae Elders could intervene on such matters. She knew, before that could come about, there would be many lives taken, harmed or twisted by one vicious Dark Fae. She would speak to her sisterkin Tara often of her concerns but Tara would simply say, 'It is what it is; only the Mother can change it but she will not intervene. It is for those entangled in Aelish's net to wake up and see the parts they have played throughout the Skeins.'

Rowan was not long for the world of man and all Shapers know her story as one of strength and compassion.

Shapers became Aelish's prey from then on. After tasting the exquisite joy she had felt as Rowan fell nothing would ever replace that craving to kill all who walked in Shaper form. Aelish however was not aware of the life of a Trueshaper whose near death would bring about her own final demise.

Chapter 39
Last Chance or Lost Chance

For those who are frail and cannot speak
...and to those who are not heard ...their voices weak
To all who mourn for what can never be
...give them your heart ...give them your energy
We all make choices ...even when we are strong
...that later manifest twisted ...somehow wrong
Send them your love without the need for show and
...with compassionate strength send love; let them go.

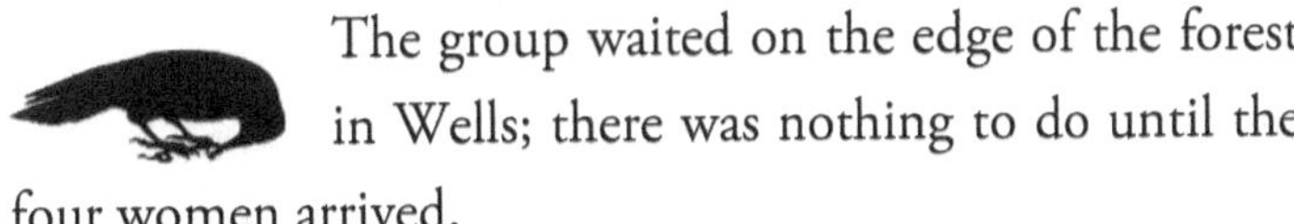

The group waited on the edge of the forest in Wells; there was nothing to do until the four women arrived.

On a parallel thread, months previously in perceived linear time, Sam felt the change coming. Faster this time, knowing once again that this was not how it was supposed to be. Too late, she saw Arianwen holding out a silver bracelet to Morgan; she knew it was hers as she fell, unable to grasp it before the world went black. This time she knew Morgan would follow her and they would meet again on the thread of the Firstborn.

For now, standing in the wings, she must focus. She felt herself flung into the passageway created by her circle of friends as they cast and the Fae who stood on the outer rim; where the Watchers kept their vigil between the worlds; keeping it a safe, neutral zone, for all travellers.

Her friends gathered for the Samhain rite and she had to remember which thread to take, which to avoid. Morgan had told her they were splitting in two for the working for Beltane in Glastonbury, and Wells for Samhain. They hadn't explained why they chose not to work at Covenstead, but she trusted their judgement.

She moved closer to the circle, remaining hidden from all but Morgan's eyes, although she saw the Fae Aerandir's eyes flicker in recognition as she stood waiting.

Suddenly she saw her friends, who should be working the Beltane ritual, step through the veil with purpose.

Beth was wrapped in her Arianwen self, wearing her mother's robe, Maeve's snood and Cal's wand. As she arrived Morgan passed her the Uilleann pipes. Her robe shimmered with otherworldly colours, seeming to flicker in and out of sight. 'A trick of the fading light perhaps,' Sam thought. Looking at Beth, she knew a complete and irretrievable change had occurred; she was no longer a simple human.

Flo carried a basket filled with herbs and a scroll, covered with tiny bird-like markings.

There they were her friends and Morgan, the only one who saw her where she stood between this thread and the other she was destined to travel. She only hoped she would find the way as Morgan patted his shirt pocket next to his heart to indicate what he held hidden there. It sang to her and she began to recognise Rowan's song.

Her friends circled. Cal and Flo, Pwyll and Claire, Lily and Max, Susan and Alex, Vanessa, Maeve and Jamie, Morgan and Beth …thirteen of the finest people she'd ever known. They chanted as they cast the circle and it became a dance, joined in by the earth, air, fire and water sprites in rhythmic movement. Sounds began to chime, the wand and snood appeared as if on fire and the delicate cape took on a look of water and air combined, appearing to float above the altar where it lay, rippling in an unseen wind.

Flo placed the scroll on the earth in the centre of their pentacle, shimmering blue on the ground and the earth rumbled gently in response.

Not a breeze stirred the forest and the air was full of ice droplets that began to freeze like pearls on every surface. Samhain, when the veils are thin and the ancestors walk the earth plane.

Once again the Fae emerged from the forest to surround their circle; to Beth's surprise they carried weapons, heavy staff and bows with obsidian tipped arrows.

Each of them began to chant the song each herb sang to them as they called for help on the journey…

Beth sang in her clear, high voice… *'All heal am I …I bring a subtle tune …like moonlight shadows reflecting in the gloom…each flickering light a story to be told …and the knowing of yourself, should you be so bold.'*

Flo… *'Moonflower bright am I and in my song …you will hear one note, which sounds all wrong …for ill use of my blessing you will feel …yet in that pain, your last …you will heal.'*

Maeve sang in husky tones… *'Sage I am …of wisdom bright …I'll guide you through the darkest night …when fear overwhelms I'll bring the light …showing the truth that blasts the blight.'*

Followed by Vanessa… *'Juniper am I, I see your soul …my task is but to heal and make you whole …see in my wisdom all that you may need …yet be warned, for your higher good I will succeed.'*

Claire… *'Mistletoe blessed am I …I bring your death when given in great supply …yet also I bring you peace …for all the notes of pain abruptly cease.'*

…and Susan… *'Centaury am I, I too bring release …that you and all your kin may be at peace …I protect those who know the way of plants …and in your word spells all desires I grant.'*

…and last of the women, Lily… *'Angelica am I, but angel I am not …I bring protection for all those who forgot …the Crooked Path that circles through the song …I will heal your notes when they are sounding wrong.'*

The women formed the inner circle and as each completed their individual chants, they continued to sing them together in harmonies that took on a haunting rhythm. Max began to sing as the first of the males, hesitantly but he became stronger as he walked the circle…

'Mugwort am I …I bring dreams true …the blessing of clarity I bring to you …though you may hide in shadows deep …I will find you in your hidden sleep.'

Alex followed Max... '*Asafoetida am I ...as Skunk-weed, known to some ...I bring awareness of the curse that's come undone ...and help to cleanse the mirk of wilful harm ...even though my reek comes not as fragrant balm.*'

Then came Pwyll... '*Wolfbane blessed am I ...I bring release ...when with your last breath, all pain I will ease ...and in that final note of your long chord ...at last the final sound, not knowing, you can ill afford.*'

Cal... '*Yarrow am I ...and together with nettle give ...to bring you freedom that you may simply live ...my harsh tonic, together with nettle take ...and then you'll see what two in one may make.*'

Jamie, shifting in and out of his Foxkin shape, sang... '*Nettle am I ...I will dispel the dark ...and in my prickly depths there lies the notes sweet as a lark ...in my green self the healing of all lies ...told to protect the fearful self who cries.*'

Finally Morgan, looking like the warrior Raven of the Morrigan's Firstborn Clan, more than ever... '*Mandrake am I, indeed you'll hear my scream ...that haunts your sleep, a harsh, resounding stream ...of all you said that disallowed your dream ...look back you'll see I'm never what I seem.*'

They circled, repeating the words and as they did, the bird-language written on the scroll began to shift, lifting off the page to take on a life of its own. Tiny Birdfae followed, hovering and swooping as they sang...

'*A flock of birds, one bird a note within a song ...each note complete, distinct within its sound ...the flock resounds, joined in winged-flight throng …but as a chord their soaring trill knows no bounds.'*

Again, they all took up the song as it became potent in their consciousness and then Jamie and Vanessa began the Foxkin song… *'I am the red, sleek moving sound …of velvet paws on mossy ground. I hear you call in deep dark sleep …and wondering, sit to watch you weep. Why do you weep, you hear me ask …you must but perform your sacred task …to live and play upon this ground …till Flidais leads you onward in the Circle round.'*

Vanessa pinned the broach to her robe and they saw her shift shape, transforming for the first time in front of them.

Morgan and Tara sang as one in husky-dark tones, a strange rhythm surging, causing the hair on arms and nape of neck to rise… *'I am Raven, Onceborn Magick, answering to only one. I watch over your tangled dreams until your work be done. Dark weaves blossom, with blood red flowers. As you come into your powers*
…slumbering deep, beware the Morrigan wakes you now from sleep …you'll find me waiting in Her musk-scented bowers.'

Flo shifted shape to sing for the Wren Clan all the other Birdfae joining her in her flight… *'Tiny bird of flitting nature, curious and bright …who takes you now upon a journey leading into light. My wings are frail, but my heart is strong …I know not the doubts of right or wrong. Listen now to my thrilling high, sweet song …until you hear me in the darkest night.'*

...and Lily... Jay bird sings a different song, collecting little gems and stones ...adorning her nest ...she now fulfils her quest ...without a need to moan ...Oh woe is me, or help me please or what is life about ...for strong in spirit, bright blue of wing she has no room for doubt.'

Flo and the Birdfae sang with her. All fell still as Claire and Pwyll circled... *'Owl's song rights the wrong of one with a shadowed past ...follow through the woodland glade, our strong wings will outlast ...the pain of life and death and fear ...our cries of warning without peer ...we teach in the darkness near ...and the shadowed web we'll blast.'*

Finally, they joined in chorus, rich and clear... *'One note ...a song corrupted by the dark ...a fallen one arises who will make her mark.*

For cursed she was and in that cursing fell ...and life became for her a living hell.

She could never hear the Mother's song ...and all her kin, affected by her wrong.

The pain she wrought in egocentric need ...went beyond the warnings of her creed.

Her clan united now, will bring her home ...to bind her, from where she will never roam.

We throw a net of song around the earth ...that healed and strong she recovers from the dearth ...of those who rob, who plunder all they see...

...our song will heal all lack ...so mote it be!'

Threads began to form around them like smoke as they sang ...some dark and others of many coloured hues.

Gossamer fine they spun out, forming a silken net that hung suspended between the Bird and Foxkin and then darkness swallowed Sam.

Each of the team grasped a thread in beak, claw, paw or hand and they flew through the tangled skeins with the elementals; they soothed the cringing dark with words of power in sweet, rich tones.

They scattered the herbs throughout the web and left trails of silvern colours that vibrated with unsung melodies to cleanse and mend. The dark passageway of broken change was like a tunnel that wove its way mindlessly through the sticky threads to the cavern of bones and feathers.

Fear and dread rose sickeningly as they felt their own part in the broken Skeins. Throughout the Tyme-space continuum, they had each had a hand in the making of the darkened weave. Maeve had failed to see her part when she'd avoided her mother's pain, seeing it only as a selfish woman's habit that needed feeding like a bottomless hollow. She had looked no deeper than the external.

Lily, seeing only her father's desertion after their mother had left, had not realised the enormity of whom her parents were. Flora had refused to acknowledge her mother's shapechanger self, but had stood strong against her arrogant father. Only Bethan, despite her unknown origins, had been clear and bright throughout her days, an example to all as she embraced her music and her Fae an-

cestry equally, yet there was for her one last thread to un-
tangle.

...and so they wove their Magick of loss and gain,
until ahead they saw the vast Tree of Blessings. In abject
sadness, they saw the dark weaving, dripping with oily
vetch and they cast their own coloured threads around it,
crying to the Mother that she help them now. Bethan
took the precious cloth of her mother's robe, offering it to
shield and shelter the gaping wound.

Flora and Vanessa mixed a paste of the herbs that
harm or heal singularly and yet combined and blessed,
would heal the wound. The great tree shuddered in response and Makers flitted, shining their eternal light into
the wound and into the body of the one who lay helpless.

Aelish, as they'd hoped, felt compelled by the music
to follow as it swept through the Skeins, waited for a
moment. Her eyes widened as she saw what Morgan held
out to Sam and knew it immediately as Rowan's amulet.
Too late, she lunged for the silver bracelet crashing into
Sam, pushing her into the Between as the threads, played
out again, repeating and reforming like the strange script
on the scroll.

Chapter 40
Final Descent

She floats on the day ...the trees bow and sway.
Never broken for long ...she can heal with her song,
Listen now hear her call ...she'll not let you fall.
Take her hand let her lead ...she has all that you need.
You'll not be broken for long ...heal with her song.
Just let go and she's there
...tender hands stroke your hair
When you're sad just give in ...feeling fragile is no sin
There's no need to be strong ...just listen ...be still ...hear her
song.

Aelish was unable to hold on to Sam, whose fiercely protective leaf sprites formed a barrier to prevent her grabbing the bangle from Morgan, which in turn kept Sam from reaching it either before she fell. Morgan grasped it and once again, the others saw him disappear, his vow to reach Sam echoing back to them.

Moving as one, they reached into the depths of themselves to throw the strands over Aelish, entangling her. Hissing and spitting Aelish fought the web of her own making, as with the influence of the Makers the black threads turned to light, gossamer strands. She screamed at the pain and the searing light as if it were burning her.

Flora almost lost her grip on the threads she grasped; she could feel the others baulk at the pain they must be inflicting. Aerandir, Lily, Morgan and Maeve held on. Claire stepped in to grasp the threads Flora's faltering hands held but Flora knew she must stay strong as Cal came from behind to steady her. Maeve held fast, teeth gritted when she knew she held the cause of Alma's and her own pain.

Pwyll came out of nowhere; blade in hand a harsh frown creased his brow. Vanessa, with her aspect Nina evident in her compassionate expression, stood in front of Aelish, hindering his access to the screaming, writhing Fae.

'I won't hurt her, Vanessa. I want to let her free on a promise to remain still and tell us what her story is that she would cause others so much pain through the ages.'

'He won't hurt her, Nessa,' said Claire. 'We can't kill like she kills and maims. It's not in our nature, even though a taste of revenge lurks bitter on my tongue, when I think of the years of suffering so many have met at her hands.'

Tara, in Raven shape, flew to sit on Claire's shoulder, muttering in bird tongue. 'I have no such compunction. I am one of the Firstborn to the Mother. What of Her revenge Aelish Farandirim? You will face Her for the final judgement of your 'gela en ardai.'

Aelish ceased struggling, falling limp as her eyes widened in fear, the stench of which was sharp in the air.

Thunder rumbled and even the Makers faltered where they worked to maintain the light in the threads.

Morrigan, Mother of the Ravenkin, materialised from the aether. Her wounded belly mirrored Silver's wounds exactly.

Silence fell to all but Aelish as the Morrigan spoke and with her words Aelish appeared to wither, becoming ancient and shrivelled. What transpired remained between the Morrigan and her one time daughter. All they knew was that Aelish would be punished enough as she worked her penance serving those whom she had most harmed, the Ravenkin.

The Morrigan made to leave but Morgan stepped forward. Eyes lowered, he spoke directly to Her, 'Mother of my Raven-self may we speak with her?' He nodded his head toward Aelish not wanting to say her name. 'She has caused such pain to so many present and who, unaware of why she did, need answers.'

'So mote it be,' she said, reaching out briefly to touch Morgan's hair. 'You are a brave and good man and I would ask you to come to live as a Firstborn should but I know you have bonded with the one known as Rowan-Samantha. You have chosen to live out this thread together and then we will see what your choices may be. Until then you are free to come and go between the Skeins of Tyme.' With that she turned, motioning to the Firstborn who accompanied her to free Aelish from the web and hold her fast.

Approaching to within a breath of Aelish, who cringed away, the group all heard clearly. 'You will give them their answers with truth and candour. This you owe them and then the Firstborn Tara will take you to your tasks.' The Morrigan shifted shape, huge Raven wings like a cloak of feathers fanned out around her; the air filled with the musky scent of Raven and she was gone.

A sigh rippled out, but they each knew their jobs were not complete; Sybille and Sam were lost, although Aelish would know where both of them were.

They surrounded Aelish, caught in bonds at her wrists and ankles. Unable to cast, she was as helpless as any human she had ever damaged.

Vanessa came forward first to look her in the eyes. 'I seek answers to my mother's death and to the spirit of Nina Giraldi's end.'

Morgan came next ...cold eyed and stern faced. 'I seek the answers to all you have done to the Shaper Rowan, to Samantha and her parents. I also speak for Samantha in her absence for why she suffered so as Magdalena.'

Cal came next ... 'I too seek answers to the shapechanger Rowan's bones and to my parent's deaths.'

Max, 'I seek answers to the aspect of myself, Eduard Giraldi, the daughter of that aspect, Nina and Samantha Raven-shifter.'

Lily, 'I look for answers to why you left us when we were children and why you would even have children if you had no love for either our father or us.' Her ice blue eyes burned into Aelish.

Bethan came last and asked nothing for herself only '…what have you done to Sybille and Sam? Why did you torture Alma and Annie Savage?' They all realised they had only thought of their own need for answers and had forgotten what had started it all in the first place; Sybille's disappearance.

Aelish recognised the weaknesses in them all, except Bethan who stood her ground calmly and despite everything, compassion still shone from her eyes for the wounded, twisted being Aelish had become.

The group exchanged weary glances as they saw their own parts in the tangled web with each question asked that was about them, rather than about those lost.

One by one, Aelish approached them in turn. 'Vanessa,' she said. 'Your mother was full of ego and self-aggrandisements. I did nothing except nurture her ego and in turn, my own. She wanted a Goddess to recognise her worth, not recognising her own and who was I to deny her this.

As to the little Nina; that is something that is not mine to tell.' She turned to Max, 'Your aspect Eduard Giraldi was Nina's father but I ask you, who was her mother?' Max looked sick at the thought of Eduard's alliance with Aelish but also understood why Vanessa had so drawn him; he'd thought of her as a little sister but now he fully understood his reaction to Nina. His daughter on another thread.

Then to Morgan and Lily, 'Likewise you must ask your father in his weakness why he was so easily led. I am but an instrument for people to see their own darkness. I was cursed and cursed in turn and the result is the tangled skein you see yourselves caught in.'

Her eyes flickered contemptuously over each of them. 'Each of you here has been an instrument for another's pain, somewhere in the web. Even your precious Sybille did nothing to stop her own sister's removal from the picture as Samantha came of age. Samantha's aspect Rowan was whom I most aimed to remove from the equation, for she stood in the way of the one man I desired,' again she turned to Morgan, 'your aspect Bran. What does he have to say about his attraction to Rowan then, even though his vows forbade it? We are untrue to our vows and ourselves when we cross the line if only in thoughts, for somewhere in the Skeins of Tyme it has indeed manifested.'

Facing Lily she said, 'Ah little fiery blue jay! I often wondered how you would be when you came into your own shape and you my son, when you realised it was your own mother to be, who you looked at once with desire in your eyes before they came across Rowan. Oh yes, I enjoyed the twist created on the Crooked Path when as Morgan you didn't recognise me, although for both of you I cast a glamour that you forget my face.'

'Wait, enough,' Aerandir stepped forward. '**Mother!**' he roared at Aelish.

Aelish shrieked with laughter. 'No son of mine are you. Look in the mirror of your kin. It will not be I who shares that truth, despite my hand in it.' She was gloating now.

'This I already know, thanks to these good people; your sick enjoyment of my pain is wasted. I know my parentage, my sister, father and all my kin. At least I am not as you have become.'

Morgan and Lily held on to each other. Lily thought she would vomit now that she was confronted by the stark reality of Aelish being their birth parent as well as Nina's, from what they gathered. Max was pale round his mouth and his breath came in short bursts as he tried to communicate with his aspect Eduard.

'Stop it,' Cal yelled at them. 'This is not the way. She,' he pointed at Aelish, 'is playing on all your emotions, knowing how she has twisted all the ties of family and friendship until they're unrecognisable. Seeking to blame each individual who wasn't even born to this thread when she played her games.' He approached Aelish, looking down on her from his great height, all trace of compassion gone. 'You will stop playing us for fools, **now**!' his voice became ice cold. 'Better yet, let me tell you what you did.' Aelish shrank away from him in a semblance of fear although he could tell by her eyes that she had heard him, however at that moment, Rob stepped forward out of nowhere. As Hercurin had appeared in Glastonbury for the Beltane ritual, so now did Robyn Goodfellow find them.

Changing rapidly, horns growing from a clear, un-wrinkled brow he spoke to them all, his eyes firmly fixed on Aelish.

'Long before I became the Spirit of Place for the Isles of Mysts, I was a man. A druid of the Dumnonii of the border country between Somerset and Devon. You, Morgan and Lily were born of the region, which includes Cornwall and the part of Wales Pwyll came from. Morgan, as Bran you were my adept and through Pwyll both you and Lily reclaimed your shaper ancestry. Bran never took the opportunity to 'Become', although he was a Firstborn, he had drifted too far from his ancestry to remember and so for a while the thread was broken.

Many summers ago in the Great Rite, The Cybil and I became lovers and we gave birth to an entity that had no recognisable origin. The Fae took her in, as Aithlin's sister, which was curious and indeed they looked uncannily alike in a mirror-reversed way of dark and light but her twisted soul, born of our love, was an unknown essence that nothing could bind by ancestry or blood in any way.

Aelish gathered souls around her who were as twisted as she was and never for a moment let them go.' Turning to Vanessa he said, 'Your mother was one of her toys, brave child and this came about by Annie's own need for recognition, her own strict upbringing was created around false loyalties through your Italian grandmother's tight, kirk orientated disciplines. She was as much a victim of bad parenting as Samantha and Maeve were. La Stregga came through her line too when all the boundaries of the Church broke free, hence her betrayal of her own acolyte Magdalena. Her eventual tortuous death, brought about by Aelish's influence through the crystal bowl that, once shattered, caused a chain reaction echoing through the Skeins of Tyme and caused the fall of Sybille and Rowan.

How we raise our children is often a product of how our parents raised us, the goal being for the next generation to be more compassionate, rather than blaming parents, who only work with the tools understood through their own upbringing. Nevertheless, I digress. We kept Aelish with us on the Isle as long as possible, trying to instil in her the qualities of the priestesses of the Seer's Isle of Mysts but her Magicks were twisted from the onset and she was cruel to her sisters and the creatures of both the physical and etheric realms.

When little Alma arrived we could see there was some sort of link and we were sure the child was not the offspring of the people who had brought her to the Isle for training. Once again, we saw Aelish's hand in the transition; never dreaming Alma was Maeve and Jamie's child from the Beltane Rite years prior to her arrival at her foster parents' home. The foster parents never mentioned her as being anything but their own child after all the waiting for a child to come. Although her arrival obviously relaxed the woman long enough for her to bear strong boys to help around the farm, giving them the excuse to move Alma on when her gifts, viewed as a curse, forced their hand. Unfortunately, greed was the other factor for a young, struggling family, to whom every penny made a huge difference to their lives. A bag of coins was all it took for them to give Alma to the Isle.' Rob stepped back, eyes downcast as he let Cal take up where he'd left off.

Cal continued, ruthlessly. 'For what you call love, you mercilessly killed a shaper by the name of Rowan because you thought she was in love with Bran, whom we know as Morgan. You shot and poisoned an innocent and a Firstborn because of your need, to be the more desirable one in Bran's eyes, although he had only a fleeting moment when you cast your glamour. He, being who he is, saw through your guile but still you used it as an excuse to murder because it was a way you saw enabled you to kill a shaper, which has been the goal from the onset. You then hid her body and stole away her familiar by also stealing the amulet that protected them both from harm.

You inveigled your way into Eduard Giraldi's heart and threw a glamour over one who should have known better;' Cal cast a glance mixed with a mixture of contempt and compassion at Pwyll who held his gaze proudly, urging him to say all the things that needed to be said and be done with. Cal continued, 'Then there's little Alma a strange, changeling child whose origins are so ancient it's a wonder she ever manifested through a human mother at all but that is only her tale to tell and Maeve's.'

He paused again his gaze, flowing over each of his friends in turn, wavered briefly as he looked to the forest edge where Hercurin stood. He nodded to Cal that yes it was time.

To Morgan and Lily he said, 'How she managed to fool you both is beyond me but then her skills with glamour are renowned as we can see.' He paused again as if waiting for something; Vanessa moved forward. She appeared to be glowing with an inner fire as she walked closer to Aelish; so close, she could smell the fear.

Vanessa's features flickered, changing shape and colouring. Nina's sweet face overshadowed hers. 'Why, Mama?' was all she said but stepping forward, embraced Aelish with compassion. As Vanessa and Nina's combined essence touched Aelish her face contorted. Another figure moved from within Vanessa, glowing with a light that grew brighter as strength and understanding returned. Vanessa faltered but the group moved in strength to support her. They each drew in a sharp breath of joy and awe as Sybille's shape appeared, frail at first but growing stronger; behind her they could make out the shadowy shape of a vast tree. At last, they sighed a collective sigh; she was still alive.

As Sam fell toward the thread she needed to grasp, pain wracked her body. Her tattoos resounded to the music from her friends, the Birdfae and from the shards of crystals held in wand and snood. They spun off her skin to form twisting cuneiform script in the air and broken, she felt torn in two; human and shifter or was it shifter and raven familiar, there was no time for thought only fear and pain. Music faded away and the thread-like tattoos held aloft. Memories surged like hot waves, just as the fires had licked at her feet when her own kin had betrayed her. Too much to bear she screamed to a cloudless sky as she fell towards the flames; lost.

When she came too, she lay sprawled on the pile of bones that had been her aspect Rowan. Something seemed to grip her and she found she was sinking into the pile. A pressure filled her chest, dust her mouth, but she fought the illusion, fighting to remain conscious.

Bones rattled and shifted, appearing to be so much more than just one frail shaper and she realised she was not on the original pile but a much greater one. She pulled her failing strength together and managed to sit up. Bones slid, rattling as they fell away into the darkness below. She was in a cairn of bones but not the one where her remains and Magdalena's ashes lay.

This was vast, stretching as far as the eye could see, interspersed with glints of silver, bronze and gold. Gathering her wits she realised they were the bones of thousands of shapers but why were their bracelets, amulets for change, left with their bodies. She knew the bracelets were the key, to maintaining their great longevity and their connection with their shaper familiar. It dawned on her then that she had never seen Tara's white winged Raven when Tara was in her physical form.

She had seen Claire's Owl and Pwyll's but had never seen Jamie's Fox when he was in his human shape either. Rubbing sore eyes, she realised there were different levels of changer, those who were pure changer, the Firstborn, who changed their very bones from shape to shape and who need their amulet to maintain it. Then there were those who needed the bird or creature familiar, in order to change. So which had Rowan been? Come to that she had never seen Morgan's familiar either.

She had made the change again now, horribly painfully, her bones stretching and changing to Raven shape after Ruark-Rowan had arrowed into her chest. So did then the spirit of the familiar reside inside after that ultimate exchange had taken place but, after the skill was mastered completely could come and go between shapes with their changer? Did it also mean that the spirit of the shaper, encapsulated in the familiar, as obviously Rowan had been, lost the ability to speak or communicate even to their kin, who they were? Why Tara had not recognised Rowan in Ruark was surprising; or had she?

'I'm missing something,' she said; her words echoed off the chamber walls and the bones seemed to shift, shimmering with the life force remaining in the amulets of change.

Sliding down the pile of her Ravenkin's bones, Sam stood at the bottom, looking around for an exit. She heard a shuffling sound as more bones moved under the weight of something. Spinning around she froze. Her parents, just as she remembered them, stood at an entrance to the vast cavern. Their eyes were cold; colder than she ever remembered them being and they were unchanged. In fact, they appeared younger than when they had disappeared.

'Mum, Dad,' Sam managed to stammer, words failing her.

They simply stared, their fixed gaze on her, unfeeling.

'You!' her one time father said coldly, while her mother circled her, a curious net in her hands.

'It's me, Samantha. Don't you remember your own daughter or is this why you were so cold, so adamant I shouldn't draw or write? Was I to become like you and your strange cult followers? Is this what I would have become otherwise had I remembered my origins?' She indicated with her head to the vast array of bones around them.

'Filth!' her mother spat at her, 'Shapeshifting filth! What have you done to M'lady Aelish? Where is she?'

'I have no idea where she is and why would I care when she had me buried for years in a cairn of bones having killed me with a poisoned dart. It's only thanks to my familiar spirit I'm here today. Or perhaps thanks to you,' she said with irony. 'Had I remembered I would be long dead I think at the hands of your **M'lady**.'

286

'M'lady is no Lady,' said a small voice from behind a rock. 'She has fooled so many ignorant into believing she was a Goddess, she is nothing but a dark Fae, a twisted one who lives to maim and kill all the Firstborn, the Trueshifters and any who are healers, Wytches and Cunningmen of the Crooked Way. All this time, since the Morrigan took you away from Samantha after the damage you caused her psyche; you've both been captured in a dark web of **Lady** Aelish's making.'

Sam's human parents exchanged glances before her mother leapt with the net to confine Sam in its sticky mesh. Alma acted spontaneously and fast, throwing herself between Sam and the net. She screamed as the trap closed around her then fell silent, the touch of the foul webbing anathema to her - the purest of spirits.

As her bright spirit left her body, returning to the waters and earth of her making, bones rattled as the whole cairn began to quake, water gushed from cracks, rocks fractured with ear-splitting rifle-shot sounds. From every nook and cranny small winged and scaled shapes emerged; Sam's leaf sprites flitted, tiny sword thorns in their hands. They flew to the net, cutting and ripping at the sticky web with the thorns; when that didn't work, they fell too with pointed teeth. As some became sick from the black ichor, others took their place, until the small body of a child revealed itself to the light of the Makers, who followed the Sprites clearing the way. They lifted her gently, reverently, carrying her away with them.

Sam's leaf sprites gathered around her and the water sprites followed their own to wherever the Makers were taking Alma.

Sam had no words for her grief at Alma's death; she could only hope the Makers were not too late. She feared for her friend Maeve's sanity if Alma was lost to her again.

Her parents stood, dumbstruck at what they'd seen. Sam had no time to think of why or how they'd become the way they had other than due to the blight. Without a backward glance, she made move to go.

'YOU!' the words came with such loathing Sam spun around to confront her mother. 'It's all because of you. You fell as a shaper and we swore no others would again. We would make sure no shaper lived to repeat the curse. The curse you laid on Lady Aelish.'

'I know of this and have been struggling to make amends, to understand what possessed me in that mo-ment...' With a slicing movement, her mother silenced her just as she had when Sam was a child. She began to chant, joined by her father's deep voice. Droplets formed on every surface that blackened and smouldered with venom...

'We bind you to eternal dark, we will return to make our mark. In truth, we curse you for your guile; believe you've won for just a while. For we curse you to live in the in-between, your voice to be heard, yet you remain unseen; forever in darkness, never free... as we do will so mote, it be.'

Sam fought with everything she had in her, with all the light remaining, because her heart had never been dark. Even when confronted by such agony, the curse forming in her mind, she'd known they were not her words, her thoughts. Even then, Aelish had managed to make it seem as if she had sent the blight that caused Rowan's fall, making it appear as a Darkmaker who dragged her Aunt with her into darkness. Like all curses, it had rebounded throughout the Skeins to cause havoc, finally to fall on the one who had instigated it and who had never again seen the daylight; caught in the in-between.

She opened herself to change, to Rowan-Ruark, to all the love, kindness and goodness her Aunt and her friends had shown her. She opened her heart to Morgan and her soul to the Lady who had birthed her, who and what she was.

Drawing the dark into her inky-black feathers as they sprouted from her head and spine, her arms became wings her feet, raven-clawed.

Flying the aethers Morgan reached out to slip a bracelet of filigree silver onto her wrist just as she made the change.

She heard screams but didn't pause to wonder what or who screamed, she embraced even the darkest corner of the universe as she became her Firstborn self and Ruark, Rowan and her familiar self, flew out of nowhere to join her. They fell together reaching out with all their merged spirit, seeking Sybille trapped in the dark somewhere.

Despite the merging Sam felt more alone than she'd ever felt in her life. She flew through the broken web pulling the darkness into her, for only by doing so, would balance be restored. The pain and horror as she ceaselessly worked her way deep into Aelish's cursed spell was beyond even the flames of the pyre. Each thread held a different secret, a darker moment, a deeper thought of what death meant.

She saw little Alma as she shrivelled to dust in the blighted web. She saw her parents taken from the weave, their lives snuffed she'd thought, because of her curse; flung randomly in the final defiant act against a dying light. Her pain unbearable, she discovered they'd been equally responsible through their gullibility and bigotry.

Agony poured through; she saw Sybille in the shock of her awakening as their eyes met, Silver looking aghast as the cause of the Maker's cocoon falling into the void became clear. Plummeting again toward the planet, not in delight at coming to sow the seeds but in horror at what the planet had become; darkness invaded. All because of one changer's fall and by one Fae, twisted by the call of power unleashed, which then became corruption. A power to defile the innocent, touched by the ensuing blight and rather die than it be their truth. Jennifer, Richard, Magdalena, Nina, all witness to the darkest weavings. On Rowan flew, her heart pounding; her breath laboured gasps.

Blinding white light flashed in the void; Vanessa stood, arms held wide, her head thrown back as Sybille's light ripped from within her. Silver came from nowhere the gash in her belly, once open to the void, was pulling in the rest of the darkness Rowan could not contain …then silence. A veil lay across her eyes; she was Samantha, she was Rowan and Magdalena all in one reconnected, triple-souled entity and then there was nothing.

Rowan felt Sybille's frail touch. Silver joined them, wings unfurled, aflame; they fell together, not into the void below but into the thread where their friends waited.

Chapter 41
Last Flight

She walks the path of the ancient of days
...as they twist and turn on the Crooked Path's way
...through the trees of the forests
...whose powers once held sway
...now diminished in the mists far away.

They woke, as if a gong had struck, sprawled on the loamy ground under the trees on the hill at Covenstead. Their circle was solid and had held firm in the energy they'd raised; the illusion of casting the circle at Wells had worked. Sybille was nowhere in sight. Sam panicked but Aerandir assured her that Sybille was in Glastonbury recovering at Chalice Well.

In silence, they closed the circle down and then Morgan and Sam stood together with Chalice and Blade. 'Let the feasting begin,' Sam called. 'Let the wine also be blessed,' replied Morgan. 'As the Athame is Male,' responded Sam, '...and the Cup is Female,' Morgan said looking quietly into Sam's eyes. 'Conjoined they bring Blessedness and Oneness in Truth,' they completed together. Sam took a sip of the Blessed wine and kissed Morgan on the lips, for the first time, before passing the cup to him. He sheathed his Athame, sipped and returned the kiss and so it was the cup passed, female to male around the circle in the ancient traditions of the Old Ways. Sam then called out in weary joy the final words, 'The Circle is open but unbroken, Merry Meet, Merry Part and Merry Meet Again. Let the Feasting begin!' She changed, bones stretching, feathers gleaming and flew with Morgan to the house.

Slowly, solemnly, relieved and shaky the team followed for a well-earned meal. Aithlin walked out of the gathering mists, a smile in his eyes as he approached his daughter. He whispered in the Elven tongue to her and she broke down.

'What now?' Max questioned, 'Hasn't she had enough to deal with?'

'Oh no, Max.' she said, reaching out to take his hand. 'No these are tears of joy. My birth mother,' she turned to Susan and Alex, 'is alive. With Aelish under the control of the Morrigan, she's waking up from the glamour thrown over her when she gave birth to us.' Aerandir's grin widened as he hugged his twin and then his father. 'Finally!' he said. 'Susan, Alex.' He said respectfully before grabbing them both in an enthusiastic embrace, out of character for the previously sombre Fae. Even Max received a warm handshake and a boisterous slap on the back.

Cal almost carried Flora to the house, despite her wriggling and complaining that she was quite capable of walking. Lily and Max united finally; Claire and Pwyll were silent, but there was a sense they would take the time later to talk through things.

Beth walked between her brother and her father, Susan and Alex arm in arm; on the peripheral she saw the Wild Hunt burst out of the forest and the group stopped to watch. Sam's leaf sprites flew off to cavort behind the Fae and Flidais saluted her Foxkin, Jamie and Vanessa. No one made mention of Vanessa's transformation but they saw the change on her as a wonderful and affirming thing.

Maeve remained stoically silent, holding on to Jamie for grim death, her eyes searching, searching back and forth around the circle, around the house. Waiting, praying, her face pleading. For a moment her face transformed as they heard a fleeting song, then silence but Maeve remained calm,

As they brought the food to the table outside, Cal lit the fire pit and in ceremony, they lit the carved pumpkins and lanterns forming a glow of light around their festive space. Morrigan returned, collecting Aelish to take to the Elders in West. She would not see the realms of Earth again, nor any of those who she'd so maliciously harmed. Despite this, she was unrepentant, believing herself justified in all she'd done. Sam's parents, brought before Sam for a final goodbye and a last chance to apologise, were unmoved; so deeply entrenched in their belief system, they too were without remorse.

It was Samhain and the veil, thin and fragile, was open for all to see what passed. They sat together, unafraid and relaxed after their ordeal and knew that whatever happened they were bonded as one entity for good. Aerandir began formally courting Vanessa in a charming and old-fashioned way, bringing her food to share from the same bowl. He disappeared for a short while, returning with flowers from his realm and a small lap harp he'd carved himself with tiny foxes and wee Faefolk. They sat as he took her through the chords again that sounded so unlike anything earthly and the carvings took on a life of their own.

Susan and Alex sat with Beth, now completely her Green-cloaked self, most of the time; she promised she would always be their daughter as she slipped away between the trees to join Hercurin for the wild ride of the hunt.

Sitting, rugged up warm against the encroaching cold, they watched the hunt ride past. In their wake, with a sob of despair, Vanessa saw Annie walking, quietly serene behind Arianrhod's pony. Sensing her daughter there, Annie paused briefly, a smile lighting her pale etheric visage and then, with a small nod goodbye, she continued her walk. A pathway opened on top of the hill in the grove and for an instant the watchers saw the Summerlands open up before her as she disappeared from view. Hercurin turned before entering; smiling at Bethan and with a salute was gone. 'Later,' she heard his deep laugh. 'Later Arianwen,' as she returned to her waiting friends and family.

Sam had taken Maeve aside as soon as she'd been able to speak of Alma's sacrifice and was surprised when Maeve's eyes clouded over but no tears fell. 'She'll be back,' she said. 'She always comes home.' A few weeks later, she announced she would be leaving for the other thread, where Alma and she had been mother and daughter; Jamie of course concurred.

Life returned slowly to a semblance of normality and the group began to go about their tasks. Max and Lily to the UK and Morgan was taking Sam with him to his little croft in the Wildlands for a while. Flora's belly grew and she took more time to walk the land with Cal and to plan for the eventual birth of their little Shaper child.

Meanwhile, Sybille lay asleep at the farm near Glastonbury. Refusing to turn anyone out of Covenstead or Earthly Rites and happy to be reunited with Robyn, Sybille remembered little of what had occurred when she finally awoke but she and Sam sat for hours working through the events of the last years and all that had occurred when Sam was a child. Sam's parents never showed their faces again.

One by one each of the team visited Sybille, reconnecting and sharing all they'd experienced, in hindsight with a great sense of awe for the success of the outcome.

Finally, it was finished.

Epilogue
Alma's Song

Where do we move between here and there?
What do we become in transition and where?
A place within of meanderings sweet or sour
…and then in sleep is lost many an hour …yet,
Summer wings enfold me and I fly
…soaring; shadow-less I soar
Winter wings enfold me and I die
…'til summer's sweet renewal comes once more.
Ancient sounds emerging make their mark;
…winter keeps her own notes in the dark.
Spring light brings the soft and fragrant tunes
…while autumn sounds her notes like falling moons
All the while, I watch and wait for you
…too sing your song in many-coloured hue
Each season turns anew upon the wheel,
…may you, in sweet transition, truly feel
…a note, a chord to sound amongst the throng
…when will you wake, when will you find your song?

 'I am that which is your bones, teeth, nails and hair; your skin dark or fair. No difference does it make to me, for you are one, in all …in me. When the element air wafts through your hair it lifts my leaves and blesses them with coolness or rips at them with taloned fingers to pull them from their last clinging, to their near dormant tree …until falling, falling they land

on my skin and become in their rotting ...one with me. Mould spoors and fungi are born from their dying. Small pelts of furry mosses cover my body and lift tiny star faces to their larger shining siblings above ...to bathe in starlight ...moonlight then closing, nestle deep within the fronds of ferns to hide from the face of my Great Son's blinding glare.

When the element of water, pours its silver weight on the boughs of my trees or pools in earthy furrows, before breaking loose; gushes thrillingly, mindlessly joyful, in their rush to reach a larger blending of their sweet and salty siblings. Always moving ...never still unless, caught by the great Blinding One in a puddle of my muddiness, they too grow over with slimy algae and frog spawn. Water becomes earth while the rest, seeping ...oozing down, down deep within my body, quenching my thirst for moisture, germinating seeds that have lain dormant beneath my skin ...like a minor itch to scratch they break the surface and are nurtured by the Blinding One until they stretch their new limbs to Him in supplication ...greening in His light.

When the element of fire ...an offshoot from the blinding one breaks loose upon the earth, all flee in fear of His heat ...and yet again deep within my hardened crust new life awaits the greening. Life force within all things is akin to this fire, hungry to grow ...no fear of change, more fearful that they will not. Yet nothing remains stagnant or still for long, when even on the stillest day, my skin is rock hard and burning to your feet. A fresh breeze can lift the heaviest hair from sun drenched, sweat-salted skin …there you have gushing from your pores, your kindred the ocean, of which you are a part, pooling in the furrows between your breasts or running down your face from soaking hair.

When you cut me, I bleed just as you do. I spill my guts to you in rich black oils, full of the fossilised bones of my many selves. My trees run red with gooey resins and sap runs in translucence through pliant stems, just as your skin runs red with blood when cut, no different to your lymph fluids, which lubricate your innards.

All these are the blood in my veins the plasma deep within my seething molten core. Hot, red; pulsing, like the blood that rushes through your heart. Oxygenated by the element of air; pumping the fiery heat, animating your limbs, your brain, your nerve endings; helping you breathe; to smell the aroma of your environment and as the fluids of saliva run, you taste the sweetness of the bounty of my body or the bitterness of your own destructive ways.

All is one, through all the bindings and blendings of these elements, no two operate in isolation, so why would you think you are alone, separate or different to any of these in your being? All run through you as they do through me …and then, Great Goddess animates us all …yes, even I have come from her …Primordial One; listen, listen and awake.' Awake she did, deep in the womb of the Mother, a tiny seed from the Birthing Tree, nurtured and nourished in the cool and dark she loved. Breaking free, her light flew to Maeve, hovering for an instant, waiting permission for she can only come again if it is agreed.

Maeve opened her heart, mind and belly, accepting her daughter in to be born again of a mortal woman.

Jamie of the Foxkin smiled…

I'm not all I seem … let me into your dream

…and I'll show you the ways between time

…but to follow me there first, come to my lair

…and trust me to answer a rhyme.

Ask me all you will, I have consummate skill

…to travel all threads of Her song.

Remember, in truth it is all by your will

…you learn which tone's right or sings wrong.

As the way becomes thin …come, follow your kin

…as they tread the roadways between

…for you're not all you seem

…and if you enter my dream

I'll teach you to shape change your skin…

Her name was Alma.

The End

About the Author

World renowned clairvoyant and a teacher of the Western Mysteries at Daylesford School of Arcane Knowledge, Penny Reilly is an initiated Bard in the Tradition of the Druid. Moving on this year to the Order of Ovate, Penny has a passion for the Old Ways of the British Isles; she will be returning there next year to carry out research for her nonfiction books and her second 'Cloak of Magick' series to come. She feels that the gentle path of the Druid, Pagan-Wytchways is the path to take for a sustainable future, connecting us to the land, no matter where we live on the planet. She describes herself as a 'nature writer'.

Her own visionary experiences are very much a part of her storyline, poetry and lyrics …this is her fifth published book. She has previously written articles for alternative magazines, blogs regularly about her ideas and way of life, writes for 'starts at sixty' lifestyle blog and has over 6,000 followers on her poetry page 'earthly rites', her school and her author page on facebook.

Penny moved to Sydney, Australia in 1980 and to the central highlands of Victoria with her husband David, 18 years ago. They share space with an 'all sorts' terrier, an old tabby cat, a small flock of hens and a fat wombat fondly known as 'chocolat', who has adopted them. Keen gardeners, they are becoming self-sufficient on their beautiful rolling acres on the Great Divide; their blended mob of children are long 'grown and flown the coop'.

You can find out more about the author, her books, poetry, and workshops through her publisher Silver Productions.

http://amazon.com/pennyreilly
http://facebook.com/pennyreillyauthorpage
http://facebook.com/earthlyrites
http://facebook.com/daylesfordschoolofarcaneknowledge
http://silversthreads.com/
http://www.goodreads.com/pennyreilly